Blood Doctrine

A Novel

CHRISTIAN PIATT

SQUARE
CORE
MEDIA

ISBN: 978-1-938633-55-3

Library of Congress Cataloging-in-Publication Data is available upon request.

This book is a work of fiction. Names, characters, places, and incidents are either a product of the author's imagination or are used fictitiously. Any resemblance to actual events, locales, or persons, living or dead, is entirely coincidental.

Published in association with Samizdat Creative, a division of Samizdat Publishing Group (samizdatcreative.com)

Cover design: Mathias Valdez, Lastleaf Printing

Prologue

The lights hanging over the young woman's head were intense. Her eyes began to water. The monitors crammed into the makeshift delivery room resonated in a chaotic chorus off of the cold, bare walls.

The nurse reached beneath the curtain. "Dear, I'm going to need you to push again."

"No," said the girl. "I can't do any more."

"Doctor, something's wrong." The nurse glanced at her, over to the machines, and back at the girl again. "What do we do?"

The obstetrician pulled the blue mask from her face to reveal flushed, damp cheeks. "We should call in a surgical team."

"There will be no one else," said the man, shifting in a dim corner of the room. His unblinking eyes fixed on the young woman on the table.

The girl issued a piercing, mournful cry as a growing pool of blood oozed from between her legs.

"I don't think you understand," said the doctor. "This woman needs more specialized care. We need to get her to a hospital."

"No, it's you who doesn't seem to understand," said the

man. "When you agreed to do this, it was on the condition that no one else would be called in."

"But she could go into shock…"

"Get the baby out of there," said the man. "Save the girl if you can, but the baby is what matters."

"Christ, she's hemorrhaging. She's got to have a transfusion."

"Doctor. The child, please."

The obstetrician pulled the mask back over her mouth. "This is on your head. If she dies, someone will have to answer for it."

The young woman cried out and the nurse nervously held the girl's hand while the doctor positioned herself at the end of the table. "Here it comes," she said, and a third surge of blood gushed out across the operating table.

"It's a boy," said the nurse.

"I know," said the man.

"After a traumatic delivery like this," said the doctor, "the baby and mother should be in intensive care." She clamped the umbilical cord and cut through it.

"Do as I tell you," he hissed.

"Is he all right?" said the young woman weakly.

"Don't let her see," the man in the suit said, advancing. "Give him to me."

"I want to see him," she said.

"That's not part of the deal," said the man.

"I want to see my son."

The man leaned across the curtain to meet her eyes. "This is not your child. He's ours, and you're never to see him."

"My baby," she whispered. "My baby boy."

"Enough," grunted the man. "Give him to me." He

grabbed the infant from the nurse, wrapped him in a near-by towel and turned toward the door, careful to occlude the young mother's view of the boy.

"My baby," she cried, stretching her arm out toward the man. "My boy!" She managed to grasp the corner of the towel as he passed by.

"Doctor," the nurse started toward the door, "stop him!"

"No," she said, turning back toward the girl. "If we leave her now, she'll die in a matter of minutes."

"But what can we do?"

"I don't know," she said, "but we should at least try something." She reached into the woman for the source of the blood. "A clotting agent? Please, what do we have?"

"Doctor," said the nurse, "you have to look at this." They stood motionless before the monitor. "Her pressure, pulse, everything is completely normal again."

"My God," she said under her breath, "the bleeding's completely stopped."

The young woman rested, eyes closed, as if in the middle of a peaceful rest. She opened her eyes and smiled groggily when the nurse came alongside her to check her vital signs.

"It was a boy, wasn't it?" she asked. "I just knew it was going to be a boy. I just knew it."

1

"Hey Nica, what's a six-letter word for 'vagabond?'"

Nica's gaze was fixed on the screen before her. "Harlot," she said.

"I thought that was a prostitute," grunted Edward, tossing a handful of almonds into his mouth. Edward was a stout man. He was also a New Yorker editor twenty years Nica's senior. Since his wife put him on a diet, Edward had replaced the M&M's on his desk with almonds. He'd eaten a lot of them.

"That's what it means now," said Nica, pulling her chestnut hair into a ponytail. "It used to mean someone without roots. After that, it referred to a male libertine."

"You're making that up," said Edward, picking his teeth.

"Over time," she continued, "it became a deprecating word for women."

Edward lifted a folded newspaper he had resting on his lap.

"New York Times crossword," said Edward.

"You just got lucky," said Nica. "I happened to learn plenty about harlots in my graduate class on women in the Bible. Do you read the Bible?"

Edward shook his head no.

"I do. I got hooked on the genealogy of Jesus. Especially the fact that there are different accounts of his bloodline."

"Uh-huh."

"Did you know that Luke actually refers to the bloodline of Mary, but because maternal lineage was not considered valid at the time it was written, the name ultimately was changed to Joseph?"

"I did not. Thanks for that."

Nica was unaffected by his obvious indifference.

"The thing is," she said, "ancient DNA samples, like the ones found in ancient ossuaries and the like, usually were traceable only through the maternal bloodline."

"Fascinating," sighed Edward. "You know you're too smart for your own good."

"Is it my fault if the average reader has the vocabulary of a seventh-grader?" said Nica.

"Of course not. But it is your fault if they stop buying our magazine. Religion mostly sucks as a subject."

At the New Yorker, where it was common practice for articles to make readers reach for a thesaurus, Nica was expected to produce detailed investigative stories. No one wanted to know about her hobbies, like when she spent three months investigating a group called The Project. They were related to the Merovingians, heirs of an ancient French dynasty, mythologized as protectors of the bloodline of Jesus. "Give it to Nica," was pretty much what everyone in the office said whenever a religion story intruded. "Priest rapes child"—Give it to Nica! "Pope calls for world peace" (yawn!)—Give it to Nica.

Currently, Nica was finishing up a story about a botanist in Israel who had nurtured a two thousand-year-old date palm seed into germination. The Israel connection made the story religious enough to get dumped in her lap.

Then there was the hokey name plate that was supposed

9

to be the "King of the Jews" notice nailed above Jesus on the cross. The Jerusalem tourist office loved this thing and everyone said it was of course a fake—until it got carbon dated. To everyone's surprise it checked out as two thousand-plus years old.

Nica had met the guy in New York who had identified it as authentically old at a conference on Biblical artifacts. He presented a paper on advances in artifact tracking using computer technology. It was not her area of interest, but she decided to introduce herself after his talk. He warmly shook her hand, said his name was Ibrahim, and the two struck up a friendship. She always liked his calls. It was usually unexpected—as it was today—but she smiled when the front desk buzzed her to say that Ibrahim was on the line.

"Nica, my dear," said Ibrahim. "It's been too long since we spoke."

"I know. How are you doing?"

"My wife is pregnant with our third."

"Wow, that's wonderful! How are the boys?"

"Fine."

"Send some pictures?"

"Of course."

"Actually, I was going to call you. I have some questions about something you have in your catalog. I'm not sure about the Latin," said Nica.

"Tilulus crucis," said Ibrahim. "Title of the Cross."

"Any chance you can tell me who took samples?"

"You never got anything from me. Understand?"

"I understand," Nica assured Ibrahim. "I won't forget it, seriously."

When Nica got back from lunch, the fax was sitting on her desk. The source number was blocked and there was no cover letter. There was also no reference to the titulus crucis on the page, only her name scribbled at the top, followed by three more names, professional affiliations, and dates. The first sample was taken in 1981, the year the titulus was discovered. The recipient was Dr. Binyamin Abijah from PaleoTech Labs, a contractor for the I.A.A. The most recent date was a month ago, registered by a man named Dr. Vaughan Pavel from the Max Planck Institute in Leipzig. The third, registered to Dr. Damian Armitage from Pennsylvania State University, was taken in June 1985.

"I'll be damned," said Nica.

"Something wrong?" said Edward, glancing up from his crossword.

"I think," she said, "I need to take a trip to Pennsylvania."

2

The dreams had been essentially the same. There was Gethsemane and the plaintive cries. There was prison, the sound of whips echoing off the stone walls. Jacob knew the scenes as if they were scripted.

In recent weeks, the dream had taken on a new sense of presence. As the apparitions became more vivid, they brought with them a salience that lingered throughout the day. Then there was the blood he woke up to, perhaps half a dozen tablespoons from each arm.

It was Friday and, as usual, Jacob was late before his feet hit the floor. He had started meeting with Father William once a week as soon as he was released from the custody of Sacred Heart orphanage. It was part of the requirement for him to receive the six-month allowance that provided for his room. He and Father William—whom Jacob affectionately called "Scratch" because of his nervous habit of stroking his unkempt beard whenever he spoke—both knew he didn't have to show up anymore, but he kept coming anyway.

His only reliable means of transportation was his Organika skateboard. Scratch had given it to him as a gift four years ago for his fifteenth birthday. Jacob still had no idea how a priest who spent most of his life within the walls of a religious bastion in northeast Denver knew how to pick out a custom deck. Aside from the board, the only other gift he had received growing up was a slightly oxidized saxophone someone had donated to the church. It hadn't sold in their yard sale, so they thought one of the children might have use for it. Jacob's slender, agile fingers had moved adeptly over the mother-of-pearl keys, and his slow, patient vibrato had manifested deep in his solar plexus, whereas many young players created an artificial tremolo with their jaw. Several of the regular men who Jacob had sat in with encouraged him to pick up a nicer horn to make the most of his talent, but aside from the fact that he could hardly keep himself supplied with reeds, let alone a new instrument, the thought of playing another sax felt like betrayal.

Jacob threw his saxophone case over his right shoulder, stuffed a folder of lead sheets and his MP3 player into his backpack, and tucked his deck under his left arm. As he pulled the door to his room closed, a familiar female voice said, "Hey, Jacob, come here for a sec."

Elena was as fair in complexion as Jacob was bronzed. Whereas her hair was fine, falling in silken strands along her neck and shoulders, his thick black hair gathered in ringlets on top of his head. Her angular features complemented the full, firm contour of her hips and breasts. Jacob was practically Elena's anatomical negative, his rangy nineteen-year-old skater-boy frame accentuated by a big nose, thick lips like ripe figs, and almond eyes so pronounced that he always looked surprised.

"What's up?" said Jacob.

"Where you going?" Elena asked. "Got a rehearsal?"

"Later, yeah," he said. "First, I have my Friday thing with Scratch."

"I didn't know you still had to go see him. Wasn't that just so they'd pay for your place at first?"

"I just—I kind of like to talk to him still, you know?"

"Cool," she said. Elena walked over and inserted her index finger through a belt loop on his jeans. "Hey, can I borrow your Miles shirt today?"

* * *

Jacob dropped the back of his board to the sidewalk, holding it in place with his right foot as he lowered the front with his left. As he picked up speed, the familiar cadence of his wheels reminded him of "All Blues" by Miles Davis.

Kaddah-kaddah, kaddah-kaddah.

Maybe he would write a tune of his own with that rhythm, he thought, something that just keeps on moving, keeps moving, moving, moving.

Kaddah-kaddah, kaddah-kaddah.

Jacob's shirt began to stick to his back where his sax case pressed against him. As he turned right again at Martin Luther King Boulevard, the church came into view a block down on his left. The stone tower was high above the other modest structures around it, with an even taller turret capping the corner.

* * *

"Whoever it is," called Scratch from within his office, "I'm busy. Unless, of course, you come bearing gifts of women or booze."

"You wouldn't know what to do with the first one," said Jacob. He propped his board and case against the wall outside the door.

"Have a seat," said Scratch, running his thin fingers through wiry tufts of his salt-and-pepper hair. He wore horn-rimmed glasses held together at the left temple by a safety pin, and his beard, thicker along the sideburns and chin while scraggly at points between, made him look like a cartoon professor type. Scratch's belly rested solidly upon his belt, causing the hole where his belt buckle was fastened to stretch three times its normal size.

"So, catch me up," said Scratch, returning to his chair, fingers tickling the edges of his beard.

"Oh, you know," said Jacob, sinking into the familiar aqua blue armchair, "same old stuff." He fiddled with the tip of his belt, flipping it over and back between his fingers.

"Priests can recite the same liturgy every week."

"I'm just working at Modulation, playing some, hanging out, trying to make rent." "What about girls?" said Scratch. He leaned forward and grinned.

"She lives at the co-op. She's a couple of years older than I am. I think she's into me, but I don't know. I get so nervous and stupid around her."

"You think too little of yourself," said Scratch. "I think you spend too much time inside your own head. Helping someone else out, especially one of those kids who's going through the same things you did, might do you both some good. Come back here once in a while and help out." Scratch glanced down. "What's wrong with your arm?"

Jacob looked down at the reddish stain that had advanced up his forearm toward the inner crease of his elbow.

"I burned myself cooking breakfast. It's no big deal."

"Are you sure?" said Scratch. "It looks pretty painful." He started to lift himself from his chair.

"No, seriously, it's cool. It blistered a little, so I put some aloe

3

"Please, Maryam," said Salome, setting a handful of dates before her. "You must try to eat something."

"How?" said Maryam, eyes still fixed on the drawn figure before her, the shadow from his outstretched arms darkening half of her face. "How can I think of sustenance when my first-born, my beloved son, suffers so?"

A sheep's mournful bleat echoed off the rocky hillside. Though the sun was hours from its high point in the sky, the leaden air already pressed down upon them.

"You are weak," said Salome. "It has been two days."

"No food," she replied, pushing the dates away, eyes still set on Yeshua, a mere boy. How dreadful life was to bless her with such a gift from God, only to tear him away.

The vertical beams to which Yeshua and the other two convicted men were bound bore the reddish-brown stains of dozens of men who had preceded them. What meager grass had dressed the earth below them now was trampled to clay. Merchants, passing on the pathway below, glanced timidly upward toward the triad of accused.

"Why must this be so?" moaned Salome, wrapping up the withered fruit and placing them in a small pouch.

Yeshua groaned. Fresh blood oozed from the puncture

wounds along his scalp, trickling into his eyes. Around his neck hung a wooden plank, attached to a narrow leather lanyard, which he had borne since the walk from town. On it, written in Greek, Aramaic, and Hebrew, was the phrase, "The King of the Jews."

"Father," he called out, gasping from the strain that his own weight placed on his breathing.

"I am here, Yeshua," she said.

"You," barked one of the legionnaires. "No talking to prisoners, or I'll have you sent back to town."

"Father," said Yeshua. "Forgive them; for they know not what they are doing."

The soldiers pulled flasks of wine from their satchels, along with figs and loaves of bread as midday shadows dissolved beneath the sun's zenith. They chewed on the rolls, sucking the seeds from inside the figs and spitting them out before gulping the fruit down.

* * *

"So what exactly does Penn State have to do with Jesus again?" asked Edward, twirling a yellow pencil between his stubby fingers.

"Could be nothing," she shrugged. "But there's a name on this log for the titulus crucis that doesn't seem like it should be there.

"How so?"

"Well," said Nica, "this titulus was discovered in 1981, and the I.A.A. tested it shortly after that. They told the public that they couldn't verify its authenticity as part of Jesus' crucifixion, and they determined it was likely a fake."

"But none of that answers my question."

"There's a guy at Penn State who is logged as taking a sample from the titulus four years after the initial testing was done," said Nica. "If the piece was a forgery, why did a professor from Pennsylvania go all the way to Israel to sample it again?"

"Maybe he was on one of those Bible tours," said Edward. "Stopped off to get a souvenir for his archaeology department."

"That's the thing," said Nica. "They have an archaeology department at Penn State, but it's pretty small, and they focus on North American archaeology. They wouldn't have the resources or the motivation to send a guy all the way to the Middle East. But the University does have one of the foremost labs for evolutionary molecular genetics in the world."

"Genetics, huh?" said Edward. "So does this Doctor—"

"Armitage," said Nica. "Damian Armitage."

"Does this Dr. Armitage work in the old DNA department?"

"Not sure," she said, glancing at her screen. "I can't find a record of him working there at all, even back when he took the sample. But it says on this fax that he was from Penn State."

* * *

Nica found a Holiday Inn just off the highway in University Park within walking distance of the Penn State campus. After signing for a room at the front desk, she ordered a cheeseburger and two light beers from the room service menu before settling into her quarters. With a full stomach and more than four hours of driving tugging at her eyelids, Nica began to drift toward sleep with the television providing the white noise to carry her off to sleep. The papers slid from her lap, causing her to open her eyes just long enough to reach for the lamp on the end table and slip underneath the polyester comforter.

* * *

Nica made her way to the campus a few minutes after eight o'clock the next morning. The central administration building was a vast colonial brick structure, outfitted with white stone columns across much of its face. A clock tower loomed overhead, lending the office building a reverential quality.

The laboratories were outfitted with the sleekest, most sophisticated modern instruments. A dozen professors headed up a team of eager students in their respective fields of expertise, and each had a lab named in their honor. Of particular interest to Nica was the Hawthorne Lab, a group focused on biological evolution. Nicholas Hawthorne guided the students through their theoretical and practical rigors, and the small cluster of apprentices worked closely with their mentor throughout their tenure at Penn State.

Nica found it strange that much of the lab's external funding came from NASA, though she read elsewhere that astrobiology depended heavily upon particular branches of genetics research for their clues about life on other planets. Fortunately for Dr. Hawthorne, his personal fascination with evolutionary biology was of practical interest to a healthily funded government program.

By Nica's assessment, this was the most likely discipline to shed some light on Damian Armitage. She sat on the floor outside Dr. Hawthorne's office, unwrapped a bagel with cream cheese that she'd picked up at the hotel, and sipped on a large cup of coffee.

A few minutes before nine, a frail mouse of a man scuttled around the corner, his face buried in the text of a magazine. His eyes flashed back and forth across the page from behind delicate wire rim glasses. He wore khakis with no belt, cuffs hovering more than an inch above his Teva sandals. He walked with quick, measured steps like someone who had worn the same path to the same door every day for years.

"Doctor Hawthorne?" said Nica.

"Hmm?" mumbled Nicholas. He rolled up the magazine and stuffed it in his front pocket.

"My name is Domenica Di Seta. I'm a writer from New York, and I was wondering if I could ask you a few questions."

"You're a reporter?"

"For the New Yorker, yes," said Nica. "You are Dr. Hawthorne, aren't you?" After an uncomfortable pause, she said, "I'm curious what you know about Dr. Damian Armitage.""Come into my office," Dr. Hawthorne said, ushering her through the stacks of journals and research volumes. "Why are you asking about Dr. Armitage?"

"I'm just trying to find out a few things about Dr. Armitage's work here."

"Such as?"

"Why he took a trip in 1985 to Israel? And why he brought back samples of an artifact that is property of the Israeli government?"

"He only mentioned it once," said Nicholas, "and he wouldn't talk about what they were involved in. Dr. Armitage was a good man."

"There's no record of Dr. Armitage anywhere in the records I can find for the university. Do you know anything about that?"

"I don't think I am the one you're looking for, Miss Di Seta," he said, staring meekly at the surface of his desk. "I wouldn't know anything about that." He glanced down at his digital wristwatch, shutting off a tinny alarm that began to sound. "If there's nothing else, I have a lab to conduct in a few minutes."

"Just one more question, if I could," said Nica, rising to meet Nicholas as he shuffled out from behind his desk. "When was the last time you saw Dr. Armitage?"

"You mean before the accident?"

"Accident?" said Nica. "What accident?"

"Armitage died in Israel on that same trip you're talking about. The last time I saw him was at his funeral."

"I'm sorry Dr. Hawthorne."

"It's just Nicholas, or Nick if you want."

"Nicholas," said Nica, turning to face him, "I do want to ask you one more question, and you don't have to answer if you don't want to."

"Sure," he said. "What is it?"

"At the service," Nica paused, "was it an open casket?"

"As I recall," said Nicholas, stroking his chin, "it was closed, for what it's worth."

4

By the time he reached El Chapultepec, Jacob was more than twenty minutes late. The rest of the quartet was already through the second chorus of "Cherokee" when he pulled his horn from its case. Ronnie Sacorello, the long-faced piano player everyone called "Sack," shot Jacob a reproachful glare. He shrugged and managed an apologetic grin, shuffling into place in front of Tucci's drum set. Diego Z., the upright bassist who they called "Zee," was concentrating on playing and didn't look up.

El Chapultepec was legendary among jazz dives, particularly famous as Jack Kerouac's hangout during his many trips through Colorado. The entire club was set up in an unlikely narrow rectangular shape, hardly twenty feet across. The dingy walls were cluttered with photographs of famous and lesser-known players. The gold-marbled mirrors behind the bar gave the illusion of more space, though no more than fifty people could cram into the venue at a time.

"Late again," said Tucci.

"Sorry guys," said Jacob.

"Let's do 'All the Things You Are,'" said Sack.

As they made their first pass, Jacob sang Ella Fitzgerald's lyrics to himself:

You are the angel glow that lights a star,
The dearest things I know are what you are.

If only he had such words at his own disposal, thought Jacob.

* * *

Celia generally kept the door to her office at the co-op cracked, but after the call from Father William, she opened it wide. The only light in the room, presented by a single bulb, gave her and the rest of the room a sickly pallor. She shifted her attention from the pile of unpaid bills on her desk to the main entrance as Jacob's silhouette passed inside.

"Jake," she called to him. "Come here a sec."

Jacob slumped into the chair across from Celia. She rolled her chair to within inches of him, pushing the door closed.

"I'm sorry about missing my shift at breakfast," he said, mopping beads of sweat from his forehead with the inside of his sleeve. "My schedule's just all turned around right now with this job, and gigs at night and stuff. I'll make sure I cover the next one."

"I appreciate that," said Celia, "but that's not what I wanted to talk to you about."

"Oh."

"I got a call from Father William today. Is there anything you want to talk about?"

"No, why?"

Jacob shifted in his chair.

"How are things with Elena?" Celia said.

"What do you mean?"

"Aren't you seeing each other?"

"Is that against the rules or something?"

"Does she have a key to your room?"

"What if she does?" Jacob said and shrugged. "You guys didn't say there was a rule against that, right?"

"Today was extermination day. We put notes under everyone's doors last week."

"So you guys went in my room," he said.

"With your permission, of course," she said. "When I went upstairs to let him in, Elena was coming out of your room. She looked surprised to see me, she was wearing one of your shirts."

"Oh that," he said. "Yeah, we borrow each other's stuff all the time. She likes my shirts."

"Look," said Celia. "It's not my business if you and Elena have something going on."

"What does that have to do with Scratch?" asked Jacob.

"Who?"

"Father William. You said he called."

"He just wants to make sure you're taking care of yourself. I told him I'd check in with you, just to see if everything is okay."

"Yep."

Jacob began to rise from the chair before she had a chance to respond.

* * *

The coffee shop was decorated with irregular strips of corrugated metal and chain link fence nailed to the sheetrock. Posters of punk legends from the eighties like the Sex Pistols, Dead Kennedys, and Husker Dü hung from chrome hooks, suspended from the ceiling by galvanized chains.

"So, what the hell?" Elena said.

Jacob settled across the table from her.

"What?" said Jacob.

"I'm in your room making sure everything's cool when I find these sheets with blood all over them stuffed under your bed. So what the fuck?"

"Yeah, that," mumbled Jacob.

"Yeah, that. Totally freaked me out, and on top of that, the co-op Nazi sneaked up on me when I was coming out of your room and scared me. So you'd better tell me what's going on."

"I don't think you'd believe me."

"Try me."

"I've told you about those weird dreams I have before, right?"

"The ones where your legs are made out of ice cream?"

"I think that's your dream."

"Right," Elena said. "Sorry."

"Anyhow, in these dreams I'm in the middle of the Bible or something. It's like I'm following Jesus around, right before he dies, and even when he gets crucified."

"Yeah, you told me about those. I guess I didn't realize you had them a lot."

"Off and on for a while," said Jacob, folding his napkin into overlapping triangles. "But lately it's been more like every night."

"So they stress you out," said Elena. "Like a nightmare or something?"

"Not really. I kind of got used to them after a while. But they've started changing."

"Changing?"

"Yeah, like, instead of watching it all happen to him, I'm him."

"Really?"

"Really. I mean, who would I tell?"

"What about Scratch?"

"I thought about it. He even asked me about it, because I told him about the first time or two I had the dreams. Since then, I just kept it to myself, with the way the dreams have changed and all lately."

"I can see why you might be worried about that with some priests," said Elena, "but he sounds pretty cool, like he'd understand."

"He might," said Jacob.

The girl with the stripe-stocking legs returned with his espresso. Jacob waited for her to leave the drink and go.

"It's more about me than it is about him," said Jacob. "I just don't really understand it."

"That's why you talk about it with somebody else, silly." Elena sipped from her drink.

"It wouldn't be so bad," he said, "except for…"

"Except for what?"

"This," Jacob said and pulled back the sleeve of his shirt.

Elena stared at the fresh wounds.

"Shit, Jake," Elena said and scowled. "What happened?"

"That's the thing," he said. "I don't know what happened."

Jacob pulled his other sleeve back to reveal an identical scab on the inside of his other wrist.

"You know what Celia would think about that."

"Yeah," said Jacob, pulling his sleeves back down. "She'd think I was trying to kill myself. But I swear, I woke up and they were already this way."

"Do you think you did it to yourself in your sleep?"

"I don't know how," said Jacob. "I don't have any knives or

27

anything around my room, and my nails don't have any skin or blood under them."

"That's fuckin' weird," said Elena quietly.

"You're telling me," said Jacob.

Elena and Jacob sat quiet for a moment. The two sipped coffee in silence.

"Do you have, like, some creepy uncle coming to visit or something?" said Elena.

"I don't have any family. Not that I know of, anyway. Why?"

"Some weird guy in a black suit came by asking for you this morning. He said he was your uncle."

5

The air inside the tomb was as still as death itself. It took several seconds for the women's eyes to adjust so that they could see the body, draped in fresh linen, lying on a waist-high shelf carved into the side of the tomb.

"There," said Maryam.

Without another word they wrapped the lower jaw tightly into place with a thin linen strip. Because Shabbat would begin at sunset and such labors were forbidden, even for the dead, the women had to proceed quickly. After placing Yeshua's arms across his body, they tucked a linen sheet snugly around the body. With the shroud in place, the women knelt next to the body, pressing their foreheads against the base of the shelf.

"Thank you for your help," whispered Maryam as the three walked toward the house of Yehudah, one of Jesus' younger brothers.

Behind the worship space was a mikvah, the ritual cleansing pool where women purified themselves after menstruation, childbirth, and following the preparation of the dead. The small limestone structure was barely high enough for Maryam to enter without bending over. Several stone steps led into the pool of crystalline water, fed by an underground spring.

★ ★ ★

When they arrived, Ya'aqov, another brother of Yeshua, sat outside the door, waiting for them. The other members of Jesus' extended family busied themselves with meal preparations outside. Salome and Mariamne started to follow Maryam inside, but she grabbed Ya'aqov by the forearm and motioned for them to wait. Ya'aqov and Maryam disappeared inside while Salome and Mariamne gathered with the others by the fire for warmth and to boil water for tea.

"Is something wrong?" Ya'aqov asked, looking out on the women huddled together in the twilight. "Is there a reason you don't invite them inside?"

"I wanted to speak with you in private."

The living space was simple but well-kept, with two rectangular rugs placed in the center of the room, surrounded by sleeping mats pushed against the walls along the perimeter. Wooden bowls and metal cooking utensils were stacked in the far corner, along with a pitcher of drinking water.

"We must make plans to move the body soon," said Maryam.

"But the man from Arimathea," said Ya'aqov, "didn't he offer the tomb for Yeshua permanently?"

"Yes, but he should lie with his family," said Maryam.

"Though he said this day would come, I always prayed that it would not come to pass. Without him here, I don't even know who I am," said Ya'aqov.

"You are Ya'aqov, son of Yosef," said Maryam, looking him in the eye and grabbing his face with both hands. "You are from the line of David, descended from Abraham and blessed with a message that will set your people free from bondage."

"It is not my message. It was Yeshua's."

30

With the table set and everyone gathered, Ya'aqov led a chorus of *Shalom Aleichem*. He gathered all of the young sons and daughters of the clan, holding them in a single embrace as he knelt among them. "May God make you as Ephraim and Menasheh," he said, meeting the eyes of each of the boys. To the girls, he said, "May God make you as Sarah, Rebecca, Rachel, and Leah." Ya'aqov rose to stand over the huddled group of children, touching each of them on the top of the head as he offered another prayer. "The Eternal One blesses you and protects you," he said. "The Eternal One shines God's presence upon you and is gracious to you. The Eternal One lifts up God's presence to you and grants you peace."

Mariamne brought forward two loaves of challah, presenting them to Ya'aqov for the Motzi blessing. Following the prayer, he handed the loaves around the circle, each person tearing a piece of bread from the loaves and dipping them in a dish of sea salt before eating them. Once everyone had taken part in the Motzi, the entire family raised their hands to the heavens and shouted, *"Shabbat shalom!"* in a chorus of thanksgiving.

★ ★ ★

VitaGen was a private genetics laboratory nestled among the rolling hills of the Connecticut countryside. Though the setting was pastoral and understated upon first inspection, something about the grounds made Nica uneasy. The manicured swatches of grass and perfectly shorn hedges had an eerily mechanical quality.

Not only was VitaGen one of the foremost forensic labs in

the United States for ancient genetics, but they also had several connections, through various newspaper and journal articles, to the Max Planck Institute in Germany.

Nica came up with the name of Dr. Max Webber as the department head for the forensic department, and had emailed back and forth with him over many weeks, developing a cordial relationship. Before leaving Penn State, Nica talked him into a late lunch meeting to discuss details of a story she was supposedly doing about the role of modern science in criminal investigations.

Dr. Webber met her in the foyer. He was a pleasant man in his early forties, several inches taller than Nica but toothpick thin.

"Mrs. Di Seta?" said Dr. Webber, extending his hand.

"Just call me Nica."

"Nica," nodded Dr. Webber. "What a pleasure to finally meet face to face."

* * *

Dr. Webber took Nica to lunch at a local diner.

"You know," said Dr. Webber, crushing a fresh mint leaf at the bottom of his tea glass with his spoon, "with the explosion in popularity of all of these crime scene shows, it seems like everyone is as interested in forensics the way they used to be into trial or detective dramas."

"Well, why not?" said Nica. "There's so much mystery and so many layers to a forensic investigation. Maybe people are evolving in their tastes beyond courtroom theatrics and brute violence."

"Makes unlikely heroes out of us science nerds," Dr. Webber

grinned. "We're not exactly used to the spotlight."

"Webber," said Nica between mouthfuls of field greens. "Is that a German name?"

"My father lived in Munich as a boy, his father sent him to live with an aunt and uncle here in the states during World War Two."

"Do you still have family there, in Germany?"

"My dad has an older brother who stayed behind," said Max. "He was already married and had moved across the border into a small village in Austria."

"Do you ever get to visit?" asked Nica.

"Actually," he said, looking into the distance behind her, "I went to graduate school there. I did some post-doctoral research at a facility in Leipzig."

"The Max Planck Institute?"

"You've heard of it?" he said.

"It's hard to do much research about forensics and not come across it," she said. "I know they do a lot of different kinds of genetics research. Mitochondrial DNA is used for identification purposes there, I take it?"

"Right," said Dr. Webber, "and nuclear DNA contains a lot more information than mitochondrial DNA. However, there is only one pair of nuclear DNA genomes—or sets of genetic codes—in each cell, as opposed to hundreds of thousands of copies in the mitochondria. So although the nuclear DNA can tell us more than the mitochondrial DNA, it's harder to find."

"So, if the nuclear DNA is a more complete set of information, then I assume that's the kind that's used for things like cloning."

"Ahh, cloning!" he said. "The hot topic of the day. Ever since Dolly the sheep, there's been quite a storm of controversy

33

around cloning. Never mind that it's been a common scientific discipline for five decades."

"Really?" Nica leaned forward. "I had no idea."

"Fifty-two years ago, some labs in Europe successfully reproduced tadpoles, though their results were not published, and no one else was able to replicate their claims."

"That seems hard to believe."

"It points to the controversial nature of the discipline," said Max, munching on the second half of his sandwich. "What's more interesting is that supposedly no other cloning projects were executed successfully for thirty-three more years, until Dolly came along in 1996."

"So the whole science of cloning stopped in the sixties and didn't progress for three decades?" Nica crossed her arms. "Given the normal momentum of scientific progress, that seems pretty unlikely."

"Depends on how you look at it," said Dr. Webber. "Some people suggest that we simply wanted to know if it could be done. Once cloning was achieved, even at a more rudimentary level, we had accomplished the desired goal—to replicate life on our terms."

"Kind of like the race to the moon," said Nica. "We went all in to get there, but then..."

"Why else would such exciting research come to a standstill for thirty-three years after finally making breakthroughs like this?"

"So you think there was a cover-up?" asked Nica.

"Not so much a cover-up as a—oh, let's call it a general lack of enthusiasm from the more well-funded governments of the world."

"Are there situations where you might have university faculty come work for someone like VitaGen?" Nica asked.

"Sure," said Max. "In fact, most of our people have some sort of university experience. It's sort of our farm league, in a manner of speaking. We recruit pretty heavily from some of the better programs."

"How about Penn State?"

"We've had a number of folks come to us from Penn, actually."

"In my initial research," said Nica, "I read through some work that came out of Penn State. Seems like a man named Dr. Armitage was a pretty big name in the field."

"That's a name I haven't heard in some time."

"Maybe you can explain to me a little bit more about the differences between the two different kinds of DNA," said Nica, trying to steer the conversation back in a safer direction.

"What would you like to know?" Dr. Webber said.

"What kinds of samples do you analyze?"

"Mitochondrial DNA. You can compare samples for a genetic match, and you can determine things like matrilineal bloodlines."

"Only the bloodline of the mother?"

"With that particular type of sample, right," he said. "With nuclear DNA, you can determine much more, but since there are only two sets of the code in each cell, it's harder to come by."

"So do all of the samples you work with have both kinds of DNA in them?" asked Nica.

"Actually, no," said Dr. Webber. "Samples containing blood, especially if they've experienced any degradation, generally contain mitochondrial samples, but not always."

"Then you could use an old blood sample," said Nica, "say,

from an old artifact or burial site, for identification purposes, but not for cloning experiments?"

Dr. Webber nodded.

"Let me see if I'm connecting the dots here," said Nica. "Do you believe that this kind of research was still going on during those missing thirty-three years, even though there's no record in the scientific journals?"

6

Several hours after he began praying, Ya'aqov opened his eyes slightly as a gentle breeze caressed his side. The stars seemed to dance in their places across the heavens. "Yeshua," he called softly. Gradually, the breeze lulled him back to sleep...

* * *

"Excuse me," said a voice. Ya'aqov's back ached and his legs were numb from the sitting posture in which he had fallen asleep. He looked up, squinting toward the source of the voice.

"Who are you?" asked Ya'aqov. Sensation began to return to his legs in the form of a thousand needle pricks. "How did you find me here?"

The stranger knelt down, his face becoming visible. He was a handsome younger man, perhaps in his early to middle thirties. He wore a week-old beard, and his dark hair was slicked back against his head, drawn together with a fresh-picked reed from the riverbank.

"Just a traveler, like yourself," said the man. He handed Ya'aqov a skin filled with fresh water.

"Where are you headed, friend?"

"No particular destination," he said.

Ya'aqov invited him to sit in the sliver of shade offered by the overhead rocks, handing him a date from the previous evening.

"I was traveling to Jerusalem, but when I saw you here, I thought I would stop and make sure you were unharmed."

"Thanks, yes," said Ya'aqov, "I'm well. It is strange to meet you this morning. I didn't expect to see anyone out here. I came here to pray alone."

"You expected to be alone."

"No," said Ya'aqov, "I was expecting someone else."

"Really?" the man asked. "Who were you meeting in a desert?"

"It sounds strange to say it," mumbled Ya'aqov, "but I had hoped to find my brother. His name was Yeshua."

"The one who was killed?"

"Yes."

"Ya'aqov," said the man, "look at me."

The identity of the man before him suddenly became blindingly clear.

"My Lord," whispered Ya'aqov. "It is a miracle."

"Are you afraid of death?" asked Yeshua.

* * *

"Edward, do you believe in God?" asked Nica.

"Religion always put a sour taste in my mouth," Edward said.

"That's not what I'm asking," said Nica. "I want to know if you believe in God."

"The one in the Old Testament who speaks out of clouds and burning bushes and banishes people for eating apples?"

Edward said. "Nah. But I think I believe there's something out there. Something, you know, that started the whole thing rolling."

"So you don't think we're just here by coincidence or accident?" asked Nica.

"Maybe it's just my own ego," said Edward, "but I hate to think this shit hole of an existence is all there is."

"Come on, it's not that bad."

"I guess not," shrugged Edward, rummaging for a snack. "But it's far from perfect. I'd like to think there's a point at which things get a little easier, where some of the suffering, cruelty, and all the bullshit makes a little more sense."

"Do you believe in Jesus?" asked Nica.

"Geez," said Edward, "ten minutes you're back and you bring the Spanish Inquisition with you."

* * *

After a cup of tepid coffee, Nica settled down with her folder to sift through the articles she had printed and the mental notes she had taken during her trip. She ran a search for Dr. Vaughan Pavel at the Max Planck institute. She logged into an online search engine for journal articles and books. Several dozen articles came up, as well as a few volumes on genetics for which he had served as editor.

Nica refined her search from the pool bearing his name to include only those dealing with whole genome amplification. Three articles remained, each written several years apart. The last, which had been published only a few weeks before, bore a heading that made Nica's neck tingle:

Blood Doctrine: Heresy or Prophesy?

Rather than a research summary in a scholarly journal, the article was an interview of Dr. Pavel for Wired magazine. In it, Pavel discussed the sample of the titulus crucis he had recently analyzed, suggesting that it was from the appropriate time period to be considered potentially authentic. From here, he described a religious theory known as the Divine Blood Doctrine, which claims that the physical blood of Christ contained—or in this case may still contain—the holy properties that made Jesus divine. Dr. Pavel had learned of the small, radical sect who adheres to this tenet following the public announcement of his intent to further investigate the titulus. Someone claiming to be part of a group known only as The Project left a threatening message on his voicemail. By pursuing his line of research, they claimed, he was attempting to play God, and he ultimately would serve considerable penance for his acts of heresy.

The author of the message did not leave a name or contact number, so Pavel dismissed it. However when he got home, the article recounted, there was a letter slipped under his apartment door. Inside were photographs of him with his wife and daughter, his sister in Austria, and his parents outside their home in the countryside outside Berlin. The Max Planck Institute, familiar with dissident voices from the religious community, promptly dispatched security personnel to monitor those shown in the photographs.

Originally, Dr. Pavel had wanted to revive the long-silent debate about the titulus crucis and its authenticity. However, upon receiving the intimidating messages, his curiosity was piqued about what this group called The Project was.

Most of the rest of the article was conjecture about the Divine Blood Doctrine concept, based principally on internet discussion forums and websites committed to the belief. In essence, those who maintain such an understanding about the blood of Jesus claim that any relic supposedly containing the blood of Christ is not only sacred, but it also still retains the divine essence of who he was. The claims of mystical powers surrounding the blood relics range from the ability to heal to containing the key to the invocation of the prophesied second coming.

* * *

"Second coming?" Nica said out loud.

"Come again?" said Edward. Nica was still fixated on her computer monitor. "Hey, that was some serious word play."

"Hmm?"

"Tell me you didn't hear that one," he sighed. "My best one all day, and you're too deep in your own head to notice."

"Sorry," said Nica, running her fingers through her hair. "Did you know that there are people who think that these relics from Jesus' life may be the missing link to invoking the rapture?"

* * *

"Miss Di Seta," said the voice on the phone, "this is Vaughan Pavel from the Max Planck Institute."

"Dr. Pavel," she said, "thank you for getting back to me."

"I understand from your message that you work for the New Yorker. I follow it regularly. In fact, I believe I read one of your articles recently on postmodernism in the church." He had a pleasant, soothing quality to his voice, clearly rich with a German accent, but eloquent and as comfortable with the language as most native English speakers.

"Right," said Nica. "I think that ran about four or five months ago."

"I found it very interesting. Do you consider yourself a postmodernist?'

"I guess you could say so. I mean, I don't put much stock in denominations, if that's what you mean."

"Then how do we delineate one set of beliefs from another?"

"On an individual basis," said Nica, "or else based upon orthodoxy. I'm afraid that the logos on the church door don't tell us much about who's inside anymore."

"I think it's a common misconception that all scientists are fierce secularists," said Pavel. "I was raised in the Lutheran tradition as a boy, and I still claim it today. Although, if what you say is true, perhaps I should reevaluate what I believe as an individual, rather than as a Lutheran."

"Not on my account, Dr. Pavel."

"Please, Vaughan will do. How may I help you Miss Di Seta?"

"I've been doing some reading," said Nica, "and I was hoping you could answer a few questions for me."

"No doubt you read the piece in Wired."

"A bit off topic, I'm curious about your decision to talk about your research in, of all places, a magazine like Wired."

"An odd choice, perhaps," conceded Dr. Pavel, "but it was serendipitous. They approached me for some information about genetic engineering and, well, one thing led to another."

"Interesting leap," said Nica, "from genetic engineering to ancient Biblical relics. I wonder if you could tell me a little bit about your interest in the titulus."

"Well," said Dr. Pavel, "as I said, my family has roots in the protestant tradition. My ancestors, several generations back, worshipped with Martin Luther himself. So I've always had somewhat of a fascination with relics of the Christian faith, and the meaning we give them."

"I understand Luther was quite a firebrand."

"To say the least," said Dr. Pavel. "He stood up for his convictions, regardless of the consequences. In addition, he benefited greatly from the advent of the printing press at the same time that he was trying to reach people with his new message of Protestantism."

"A beneficiary of technology," said Nica, "not unlike you."

"I suppose so," said Dr. Pavel, "though my work is hardly as earth-shattering as Luther's."

"So what exactly was your purpose in taking a sample of the titulus?"

"As you likely already know," said Dr. Pavel, "most relics attributed to Christ are under the control of the church. It's not exactly easy to walk into a Spanish or Portuguese cathedral and convince the presiding priest to hand over his most sacred relic to a scientist."

"Plus," said Nica, "if they let you test all of these relics and found them to be frauds, they'd have nothing."

"A bit of a cynical way of looking at things, but that is true," said Dr. Pavel.

"You don't think it matters whether or not they're being lied to?" asked Nica.

"That would suggest there was a conspiracy involved," said Dr. Pavel. "I think, in most cases at least, that the leadership of the church believes in the sacredness of these relics."

"So why are members of The Project threatening your life," said Nica, "as well as the lives of those you love?"

"Faith is an odd thing," said Dr. Pavel. "By definition, it is not based on rational, analytical reasoning. Science is engaged in measuring observable data. That is, we're concerned principally with those things we can engage with our senses, either directly with the so-called naked eye, or with the use of technology. Since we cannot see, hear, smell, touch, or taste God—though some might debate this—it is beyond the realm of science."

"Based on that logic," said Nica, "it seems like religious leaders would have nothing to worry about with respect to science."

"If we were so compartmentalized," said Dr. Pavel, "that we could either be entirely faithful or entirely rational, this might be so. However, we are remarkably complex. Without the human imagination and a sense of mystery, we would not have theoretical fields of science, which often lead us to the most profound breakthroughs we have ever had."

"So you believe it takes faith to be a good scientist."

"Absolutely," said Dr. Pavel. "If you limit yourself to pure empiricism, you are nothing but an elaborate computer. It is in the human capacity for both rational thought and faith that we find our place in the universe."

"Maybe I'm missing something," said Nica, "but it seems to me there's nothing threatening whatsoever about your research."

"Oh?" said Dr. Pavel. "Why is that?"

"Well, regardless of what you determine about the age of the titulus, there's no way to place it at the actual crucifixion of Jesus Christ."

"There are samples which would make for interesting comparative research," said Dr. Pavel.

"You mean the relics in the churches?" said Nica. "Didn't you already suggest that those haven't been proven to be authentic either? If, in fact, there was blood on more than one relic, and if the samples didn't match, the only thing that would prove is that they weren't from the same person, right?"

"That is correct."

"Then there would have to be something else," said Nica. "Something more compelling to make the case that this actually was the blood of Jesus of Nazareth."

"That is correct."

"But what?" Nica asked. "What do you know that you're not telling me?"

"I'm sorry," said Dr. Pavel, "but as much as I have enjoyed our conversation, I must let you go. I don't want to bring any harm to you."

"Harm to me? Are you saying that your interest in the titulus is why The Project is after you?"

"I did not say that, per se."

"And are you suggesting there actually is another way to verify that your sample is the real thing?"

"It's been a pleasure, Miss Di Seta," said Dr. Pavel, "but you must please excuse me."

"If there's something to all of this that people are willing to kill and die for," said Nica, "you've got to give me more than this."

But the line was already dead on the other end.

7

"So," said Jacob, "how are you?" Elena purred and nuzzled into his side as they stretched across her bed. The warmth of her naked body radiated against his exposed skin. He resisted the urge to turn toward her and pull her to him, resigning himself to the giddy satisfaction of their intimate embrace.

"Hungry," whispered Elena. "I want French toast."

"Well, I did get paid last night, so if you want, we can go down to the Walnut Street Café."

"Only problem is," said Elena, "that means we'd actually have to get up." She kissed along his ribcage, making her way up to his neck, earlobe, and eventually his mouth. Jacob ran his fingers through her hair, staring into her eyes.

"Maybe in a little while," he said. "I'm in no hurry."

"Me either." The two of them drifted languidly in and out of sleep until a clamor from across the hall caused them to stir.

"What the hell," said Jacob, sitting up. "Did that come from my room?"

"Sounded like it," said Elena. "But who would be over there? Does anyone else have a key to your room?"

They could hear a banging sound coming from what sounded like his room. Jacob got up and looked down the hall. The door to his room stood open. He walked into the hallway and stared through his door. A few albums and articles of clothing had been scattered violently. As he took a few steps into his room, he heard footsteps in the hallway. He turned, only to catch a figure in a dark jacket disappearing down the stairwell.

Jacob ran toward the top of the stairs, then retreated, suddenly aware of his nakedness. By the time he snatched his jeans from Elena's floor and wound his way down the staircase, the man was out the door.

"Did you see anybody?" she asked, peeking out from her room.

"Some guy," Jacob said, flopping back-first onto her bed. Elena rested her chin on his stomach, her hand against his side.

"Who," she said.

"Don't know."

"Did you see him carrying anything?"

"No," said Jacob, easing her head onto his lap and grabbing his shirt. "But I didn't get a very good look either." Elena grabbed a pair of shorts to conceal her lavender panties, and a Super Mario T-shirt off the top of the clothing basket at the foot of her bed.

"Well, we know your horn is safe, 'cause you never took it back to your room last night." Elena pointed to the case in the corner next to the bed. "We'll go look through your stuff together," she said, placing her hand in his.

* * *

Every drawer in the room had been emptied into the middle of the floor, and the few shelves of books were bare, their contents scattered along the far wall beneath the window. The mattress was leaning against the box spring, and both had been shredded from top to bottom. Jacob went straight over to his record collection, setting them upright, pushing a few back into their sleeves. Silently, Elena slid each of the dresser drawers back in their place and began folding his clothes, setting them in piles on top of the dresser.

"Don't worry," she said, "you can sleep with me until you get another bed."

"Thanks," Jacob smiled. "At least something good can come of this."

"What the fuck?" said Allen, poking his head around the corner. "That weird guy in black do this? I thought he was looking for you, somebody from the club or something… Did he get your horn?"

"From what we can tell," said Elena, "he didn't take anything."

"What an asshole," said Allen. "If he's gonna trash your place, at least he could take something."

"Are you high?" asked Jacob.

"Nah, just bummed. I tried to lift the guy's wallet when he ran into me down in the lobby, but he was a slippery fucker. I came by to see what's up."

"So you didn't get anything off him?" asked Elena.

"Just some piece of paper."

"What kind of paper?" said Jacob.

"You know," said Allen, "flat, kind of a rectangle."

"You idiot," said Elena, "not the shape. What was it, and where the hell is it?"

"I dunno," shrugged Allen. "Tossed it. It wasn't money, so what do I care?"

"You threw it away downstairs?"

"In the kitchen, yeah," said Allen. "It was nothin' though.

48

Just a plain old piece of paper."

"Show us where you put it," said Jacob. Allen took them down to the large, gray industrial trash bin inside the door to the kitchen.

"I put it in there, I think," he said.

"You think," said Elena. "You took it from the guy five minutes ago and you can't remember for sure where you put it?"

"Dude," he said, "it was totally orange. I remember now."

"God, you're a tool," said Elena. She came alongside Jacob, looking over his shoulder. "It's a receipt, looks like for dry cleaning."

"But there's no name on it or anything," said Jacob. "No credit card number. No signature."

"Yeah," said Elena, "but it looks like this is the one they gave him when he dropped his stuff off. Maybe if we go there with this receipt, we'll figure something out about who this guy is."

"Hang on," said Jacob, "why don't we just call the police?"

"Police won't do shit," she said. "We can't prove he took anything. I mean, what are they gonna charge him with? Pulling the tags off your mattress?"

"It is a federal offense," Allen said. Elena rolled her eyes.

"What about breaking and entering?" said Jacob.

"Yeah," said Elena, leaning against the counter, "but if he didn't take anything, how motivated are they gonna be? We should look for him ourselves and try to figure out what he was looking for."

It was a dozen blocks from the café to Speer Avenue. Elena and Jacob picked up the Cherry Creek trail on the way to the cleaners. Manicured lawns, colonial Denver Square homes with white pillars across the front, and flawless automobiles with equally flawless drivers adorned the thoroughfares. Jacob avoided looking these members of the social elite in the eye, though Elena was unfazed.

"There," said Jacob after passing several more Range Rovers and dogs in designer sweaters. "That's the place on the receipt." They climbed the stairs and entered the dry cleaning store, which smelled of the lingering essence of bodies, cleaning fluid, and potpourri. The concoction made him slightly nauseous.

"Yes?" the woman behind the counter said curtly. Jacob pushed the receipt across the counter toward her and she snapped it up. She reached for the clothing carousel controls behind her without looking. She turned just as the black suit rounded the corner.

"Leaving town ahead of schedule, Mr. Miller?" the woman asked, glancing first at him, and then the suit, which was several sizes too large for him. "We had this scheduled for delivery to your hotel later this afternoon."

"Thanks," Elena smiled, "but that won't be necessary." As they returned to the street with the suit, Elena pulled the receipt from the hanger.

"There's the mother lode, right there." On the receipt was the name Haman Miller, the note, "PAID – cash," scrawled in the corner, and the address for the Ambassador Hotel in downtown Denver printed at the bottom. "Let's go see what that creepy old fucker is up to."

* * *

A thin shaft of light cut across the hotel room, disturbing otherwise total darkness. The man sitting on the side of the bed was wrapped in shadow, hands on knees, as still as a corpse. The only signs of life in his emaciated, necrotic body were his constantly darting eyes, shifting between the clock on the nightstand and the phone. As the time clicked past one in the afternoon, his knuckles tightened, draining their color to a pale yellow against the dark fabric of his loosely hanging slacks. The phone had not completed its first ring before he picked it up.

"Miller here...Yes, sir...Just this morning, sir. No, sir, no harm to the young man." The man ran his finger along the seam of his pants as he listened to the voice on the other end.

"Well, sir," he said, "I may have found something. Blood, on the sheets," then silence. "Quite a bit, but I can't confirm it was his." He nodded as the instructions came. "No, sir, not until instructed."

He stood up, pacing the few feet the tangled phone cord would allow. "Yes, sir, I did get a sample. It was sent express just before noon today." Another pause. "I believe he saw me leaving, but we've had no direct contact." He grabbed a slip of paper from the nightstand and scribbled down a note to himself.

"Got it," he said. "No, sir, no questions." He hung up the phone, taking in a long breath. Then he turned toward the shaft of light in the window, knelt against the side of the bed, bowed his head, and closed his eyes.

* * *

Damp with sweat, Ya'aqov burst through the entry of Yehuda's home. He stumbled over a pair of copper kettles set by the opening. He cursed in frustration. Then his eyes adjusted to the indoor light. Yehuda and Maryam were staring anxiously up at him.

51

"Well," said Ya'aqov, facing her, "what is it, then?"

"It's Yeshua," said Yehuda. "His body has disappeared."

"I don't understand it," Maryam shook her head. "We went to complete the preparations, and the stone was rolled back. Inside, the tomb was empty. I saw the tomb myself, and even the linens in which the body was wrapped were still there."

"Ya'aqov," Yehuda said. "There's more." Ya'aqov stared at his brother.

"In the days since Shabbat," said Maryam, "some things have happened that are difficult to explain. When we left the tomb," said Maryam, "we were met by two men dressed in brilliant white clothing. They explained that Yeshua had been raised, as was prophesied." Ya'aqov sat in stunned silence as Maryam continued, "We joined the men to tell them the news, but they only laughed at us. Only Cephas went to the tomb to see."

"But then," said Yehudah, "Cleopas and Simon encountered a man along their way to Emmaeus. Though he did not reveal himself as such at first, they vowed upon their own eyes that it was Yeshua himself."

"And just yesterday," said Maryam, "Yeshua dined with the men here in town. He led them out to Bethany, blessed them, and then he was gone." Maryam's eyes glistened with a mixture of grief, joy, and utter amazement. "Honestly, Ya'aqov, my heart cannot bear all that has happened in these recent days. I don't know what to make of it." Ya'aqov held both of Maryam's hands in his, pressing them against his forehead.

"Mother," said Ya'aqov, "I understand."

"How can you?" said Maryam. "When I don't even understand what I've just told you?"

"Because I have seen him as well."

Though the absence of the disciple—the one who had kissed Yeshua on the cheek moments before his arrest—was obvious, no one spoke of it openly. His body had been found, alone, clutching a small satchel of coins that had been his compensation for the act of betrayal. The price of a slave, some had said, was what he had been paid.

The room was buzzing with muted whispers, punctuated occasionally by shouts of frustration.Women floated around the perimeter of the space, quietly filling cups and exchanging anxious glances. An awkward combination of fear and excitement stirred among them until Ya'aqov broke the tension.

"My brothers," said Ya'aqov, raising his hand, "it is good to see you all again. I have called you here because we have been witness to amazing events in these past few days." His words were followed by a swell of close conversation among the disciples, some shaking their heads, others wringing their hands in distress as they glanced nervously toward the door.

"It is too soon," said Shimon, shifting nervously. "We should not be gathered like this, right in the middle of Jerusalem." Several of the disciples nodded in agreement. "Ya'aqov, we appreciate what you have been through, as have we all. But calling us together while Pilate and his men are so eager to seize Yeshua's followers is dangerous."

"Shimon," said Ya'aqov, "I know you saw the miraculous appearance I have heard about." Shimon stared silently at the floor. "Were not all of you witnesses to the very same thing? And yet here you sit, concerned about your own skin, fearful of the consequences of even speaking of Yeshua."

"It is true," said Cephas. "We did witness a miracle, and we praised the Lord for this great gift. But now, we are unsure of what to do next."

"You share your story," said Ya'aqov plainly.

"With whom?" asked Shimon.

"It was one thing to follow him when he was alive," said Johannon, "but entirely another to take hold of this ministry ourselves and continue where he left off." Ya'aqov stood in the middle of the circle of men, turning slowly to face each of them.

"Then go," said Ya'aqov. "Return to your villages, and go back to the trades you once knew."

"But how can we?" said Cephas. "After what we've seen, and what we've heard? I could never return to the life I knew before."

"Why not?" asked Ya'aqov.

"Because I am no longer that same man. I have become someone else."

"And who is that?"

"A vessel," said Cephas. "We all are vessels."

"And what is more valuable," said Ya'aqov, "the precious contents these vessels bear, or the fragile shells that hold the contents? You few possess a priceless knowledge, one that would turn the world on its end. Yet you would keep it to yourself to save your own necks." Ya'aqov turned as if to leave.

"Wait," said Cephas. "He is right. If we give up now, we have learned nothing." He turned back to Ya'aqov. "So, what do we do with this knowledge?"

"We go," said Ya'aqov. "We speak with authority, no matter the cost. When I was in the desert, I too had an encounter with my brother, Yeshua. He shared with me a vision. Our journey is not yet complete, and the work he began is far from done.

What you do with this charge, I cannot tell you. That is for each of you to decide."

"No matter the cost," said Johannon, rising to stand with Ya'aqov.

"No matter the cost," said Cephas, standing alongside them. Mariamne, who had been sitting in the shadows of the great room, broke through the circle, placing her hand on Ya'aqov's shoulder.

"No matter the cost," she said.

* * *

Ya'aqov and his brother Yehudah sat around the glowing embers of the evening fire with Cephas, Mariamne, and Johannon. They laughed and shared stories like lost friends who had been rejoined after years apart. As the evening waned, stories and gentle taunts gave way to fatigue, each settling by the fire until only Cephas and Ya'aqov remained awake. Cephas issued a hearty yawn, which then spread to Ya'aqov, and then back to Cephas again.

"See the power you have over me?" said Ya'aqov, rubbing his eyes.

"I have no power," said Cephas. "I am only a simple man with simple beliefs."

"From what Yeshua shared with me in the desert," Ya'aqov said, "you have quite an important role to play in this movement of ours."

Cephas stared into the fire. "Me? I have a hard enough time stringing a handful of words together. I'm no leader," said Cephas, shaking his head in embarrassment. Ya'aqov's laugh stirred the others momentarily, and then the two men leaned against the stones around the circle, searching the heavens as their eyes slowly gave in to sleep.

"Ya'aqov," said a woman's voice from behind his head. He felt a hand prodding his shoulder as he rolled over from his prone position against the rock. As his eyes cleared, he saw a wide-eyed Maryam standing over him.

"What is it mother?"

"I had a dream last night," said Maryam. "Yeshua came to me at the family tomb. When I awoke just before dawn this morning, I felt drawn there, so I went."

"Alone?" asked Ya'aqov, pulling himself to his feet. "It's not safe for you to travel by yourself, especially now."

"Never mind that," said Maryam. "When I got there and went inside, there he was."

"Who, Yeshua?"

"Yes," nodded Maryam. "It was him, wrapped from head to toe and adorned with fresh spices."

"You found his body," said Ya'aqov. "For a moment, I thought you meant he spoke to you as well."

"No," said Maryam, "though I confess I no longer understand the differences between the worlds of the living and the dead. All I know is that it was Yeshua. I ran as fast as I could back here to tell you." Maryam clung to Ya'aqov's arm. "My son, what do we do? Shall you come with me to the tomb?"

"No," said Ya'aqov, "there is nothing for me to see there. If Yeshua has something to reveal to me, I'm sure he'll meet me wherever I am." He stirred the ashes from the fire, searching for any lingering embers. "The others will be awake soon. We should prepare a meal. There is much work to be done."

8

"**D**ammit!" Nica dropped the phone into its cradle, sighing as she slumped in her chair.

"What?" said Edward.

"This guy cut me off before I could finish with my questions."

"So go see him."

"He's in Leipzig," said Nica.

"Maybe he was just in a hurry. Try calling him back in a day or two."

"I could tell I was close to a nerve," Nica said, shaking her head.

"Maybe it's just not meant to be," shrugged Edward.

Nica stepped behind Edward to see what he was working on and spotted a yellow sticky note clinging to the side of his screen. "Dr. Armitage" and a phone number were scribbled on it.

"What the hell is this?" she said, peeling the note from off the monitor.

"Oh, yeah," said Edward, "Sorry, I meant to give that to you when you came in. Some guy called for you just before you got here."

"Are you messing with me?" asked Nica, sticking the piece of paper to his forehead.

"Hell," said Edward, peering out from beneath the yellow slip. "I just forgot. Why, is he important?"

"You could say that, yeah," said Nica, sitting on the edge of Edward's desk. "He's dead."

★ ★ ★

The number was linked to an answering service. When Nica identified herself, the woman on the other end nonchalantly rattled off her instructions.

"Dr. Armitage has asked to meet with you this afternoon at two o' clock at The Grindhouse, four blocks from your office. Shall I tell him you're available?"

"Yes," Nica said, "please do."

That was it. The woman sounded as if this were just another answering service call, no big deal. Nica wondered if it was a joke.

★ ★ ★

The Grindhouse was a burger joint operated by a friend of Nica's cousin, a guy named Frederick. He had gone to film school at NYU for a year and a half and then dropped out. A fan of the classic exploitatively violent grindhouse horror film genre, he outfitted the entire space with paraphernalia from scary B-movies. Despite the camp, Nica enjoyed the place.

When Nica came through the front door, a handsome man in his late forties or early fifties raised his eyes to meet hers. He was sitting across from the door under a poster of a hatchet wielding man holding a severed head in one hand. The top of the table was like a glass box and in the case was a hatchet, a coil of rope, and paint splashes meant to look like blood.

"Miss Di Seta," said the man, "I'm a fan of your work." He stood to shake her hand. "Thank you for coming to speak with me on such short notice. As you can probably understand, I don't have the luxury of making appointments too far in advance."

The man had the bronzed complexion of someone who spent more time out of doors than in. That, or he was some sort of tanning salon nut. Either way, he was handsome. He had a few lines around his eyes and the corners of his mouth, but his pronounced cheekbones and strong jaw line completed the handsome outdoor man look.

"You can imagine my surprise when I heard from you, Dr. Armitage," said Nica, trying not to stare.

"Thought I would be older?" he smiled. He held out his hand. "Hi Nica, call me Damian."

"Yeah," Nica said, "something like that...Damian."

"I was only twenty-six when I went to Israel," Damian said.

"Wow," said Nica.

"Plenty of scientists realize their greatest achievements before they are thirty. I didn't have much of a chance to follow through on any of my longer-range plans before things got... complicated."

"And by 'complicated,' you mean attempted murder," said Nica.

"Attempted murder?" said Damian, tracing the outline of a hatchet beneath the glass top of the table. "There was no attempt on my life. Not yet, anyway."

Damian waved to a woman behind the counter, who pointed at what looked like an old speaker from a drive-in movie lot, bolted to the wall in their booth. Next to the speaker was a red button, and above it a sign read, "Order here; ask about our slasher special." He leaned toward the speaker and ordered a John Wayne Gasey with cheese and a side of fries. Nica had her usual: the Grindhouse burger medium rare.

"I'm sorry," said Nica, "I'll set aside the irony of having a conversation with a guy who's supposed to be dead, but there're so many questions."

"Fire away," said Damian.

"Okay," said Nica, "let's start with why you went to Israel."

"I was doing post-doctoral work at Penn State," said Damian. "My focus was on evolutionary molecular genetics—E.M.G. Even though the department focused on North American finds, I had a personal interest in Middle Eastern artifacts."

"So how did you end up at Penn State?" asked Nica.

"Pretty simple," said Damian. "They offered me a full ride. The prospect of getting through my Ph.D. with no debt was enough to change my priorities. But in the meantime, I kept up with all the finds in Palestine. Then during a break between semesters, this woman from the university's Board of Regents came in and started talking to me."

"They had the money, and you had the know-how?"

"Not dissimilar from most any university system, really," said Damian. A waitress set their drinks in front of them. She had fake gashes on her wrists. "The woman from the Board asked me if I'd be interested in a special assignment for the university. I explained to her that all of my projects come from the department head, but she told me this was a special situation and that I would report directly to the regents."

"That's strange," said Nica.

"I thought so, too," said Damian, "but she explained that there was a donor who was willing to make a very sizable donation to the university if we would carry out some research."

"Pretty tempting," said Nica.

"It was," said Damian. "A week later, I was on a plane to Tel Aviv."

"I assume this was 1985," said Nica, "and that you were sent to take samples of the titulus crucis."

"They wanted me to secure a sample that included organic material in order to compare it to an existing sample."

"Organic material?"

"In this case, blood," said Damian. "I tested the first sample before I left and found it curious that it was a bone sample."

"So you knew what the titulus was," said Nica, "and you knew your comparison sample was something other than a sample from the same thing."

"Unless by some freak coincidence the titulus contained bone fragments as well."

"It seems like they were taking a big risk," said Nica. "I mean, assuming they wanted to keep it secret."

"They were very clear about the confidential nature of the job," said Damian, "but there is no way someone without the proper credentials could get into the I.A.A., let alone take samples out with them. And even if they could, the type of equipment necessary to perform E.M.G. analysis isn't exactly available in every lab in the country."

"I still don't understand how you ended up dead but not dead, and why Penn State seems to have no record of you in their systems."

"If they thought the titulus was authentic, they must have had reason to believe that the bone sample was from the same source. I figured I'd take a side trip to Jerusalem since I was already in Israel. In 1980, the Tomb of the Ten Ossuaries had been discovered there, and if they thought enough of their samples to send me all the way to Israel, I figured it was worth a look."

"You went to the Jesus Tomb?" asked Nica.

"That's what it's called," said Damian, "though that claim is strongly challenged."

"Then why did you go?"

"I had a few questions."

"Did you actually get to go inside the tomb?"

Damian shook his head. "The next day, while I was out for dinner, my hotel room was ransacked, and the sample from the titulus was stolen."

"But that doesn't mean anything for sure," said Nica. "There are theives all over that area. Antiquities like that are valuable on the black market."

"True," said Damian, "but I doubt if bandits leave photographs of family members, along with threats on your life and your loved ones if you return home."

"Holy shit!"

"So to speak. So there I was, stuck thousands of miles from home, no money, no friends or professional contacts, scared shitless. I called the airline to reconfirm my ticket, and it had been cancelled. I tried to call in to the phone system at the university, and my password didn't work. Even my phone number at my apartment had been disconnected."

"My God," said Nica. "What did you do?"

"Next day I read in a sidebar in one of the English language Israeli papers that my body had been found in a car that had exploded outside of Tel Aviv."

"I've read *The Da Vinci Code*. I know how this sort of conspiracy goes."

"No," said Damian, "not exactly. It does involve a religious group though, or groups, I should say."

"Like a conspiracy theory?"

"Not exactly," said Damian. "There is a man—an Egyptian—named Hamadi Chamoun, who is the heir to an oil fortune. His family has connections to the Lebanese Chamoun Family, whose patriarch, Camille, was the president of Lebanon in the fifties. Camille was also the principal leader of the Christian movement in Lebanon during the Lebanese Civil War, which came thirty years later." The waitress with the slit wrists slid two plates of food in front of them.

"I'm familiar with Camille," said Nica. "He was a big champion of Lebanese independence, right?"

"That's him," said Damian. "He was enamored with Christian mysticism, particularly the ancient monastic group called the Essenes. It was perfect for a romantic like Hamadi. There is relatively little known about the Essenes, so he is free to fill in the blanks with his imagination. He pored over the writings of people like Flavius Josephus, which led him to the Dead Sea Scrolls."

"Which were written by the Essenes," said Nica.

"Supposedly," said Damian. "They were found in the caves of Qumran, outside of Jerusalem, back around the time when Camille Chamoun was the Lebanese president."

"Interesting coincidence," said Nica.

"Coincidental to you and me," said Damian, "but for Hamadi, this was some sort of sign. He determined that his family was descended from the Essenes, and that he was ordained by God to carry on their legacy."

"Their legacy?" asked Nica. "I thought the Essenes were Jews and that Hamadi was a Christian."

"The Essenes apparently were hard to define by any particular Abrahamic faith tradition. They were a discipline unto themselves, adopting parts of Judaism, early Christianity, and other mystical practices into a unique ascetic culture. After finishing college in Europe, Camille went on a pilgrimage to Qumran, and when he returned he claimed to have received a vision from God."

"Wow," said Nica. "So this rich kid from Egypt goes on a vision quest and comes back with a divine mandate."

"He's really something," said Damian, "but his charisma can't be understated. He's a very compelling figure."

"So people believed him."

"Enough to convince him that his vision was legitimate," said Damian.

"Nica," a voice came from over her shoulder. Nica turned and found Frederick, the Grindhouse's proprietor, leaning against the back of her booth. He wore a faded T-shirt bearing the logo for the post-apocalyptic zombie film, 28 Days Later, with the quote, Your days are numbered, scrawled across the bottom.

"Frederick," Nica stood to give him a hug. "How have you been? You look great." Frederick shrugged and looked around the room.

"Hey, you know, business is pretty good. Can't complain."

"I see you've added some flair to the waitresses," said Nica. "Slit wrists, bullet holes to the temple, very…"

"Appalling?" said Frederick.

"I was going to say unique," Nica said, "but appalling works." Frederick grinned.

"I figured I'd put the stuff I learned in my special effects class to some kind of use," he said.

"Sorry," said Nica, "Frederick, this is…" Damian interrupted before she could finish.

"Jason," he said, rising to shake Frederick's hand. "Jason Silverman. Pleasure to meet you."

"Right," said Frederick, "yeah, likewise." He turned to Nica. "Hey, we're having a little thing next Friday at my place. You should drop by for a while."

"Sure," she said, "sounds like fun. I think I'll be around."

"Nice kid," said Damian after Frederick walked away. "Sorry about the name thing. But this sort of public meeting is a rarity for me."

"No, I understand," said Nica. "You were saying?"

"As soon as Camille came back from Qumran, he claimed that God told him to build a church, and that he was to be the priest of the new order he would establish there."

"Was this like a new denomination?"

"He saw it all as a fulfillment of prophecy."

"So he considered himself to be a prophet?" said Nica.

"Well, he considered himself to be the catalyst, of sorts, that would bring the claims of the Biblical prophets to realization."

"This guy sounds insane," Nica said.

"Could be," said Damian, "but he was intelligent, rich, powerful, and he had a way about him that made people want to follow him. And crazy or not, he still has this same sway over many others."

"And what's the prophecy he's supposed to help fulfill?" asked Nica.

"The Second Coming."

"You mean this guy thinks he's the reincarnation of Jesus?"

"No," said Damian, "but he believes that he's an emissary. He claims that he is responsible for hastening the rapture."

"And now it's his job to push the timeline along," said Nica.

Damian nodded. "He manipulated the regents at Penn State with a big gift to the school if they would help him get his hands on a sample of the titulus."

"I follow you," said Nica, "but if they had to get you to secure the titulus sample from the I.A.A., how were they planning to get bone or tissue samples from the ossuaries? If I'm not mistaken, those are housed at the I.A.A. as well."

"You're right," said Damian, "However, they don't contain the bones themselves. The only organic materials left in the ossuaries are remnants from a time when they were stored there before they were moved."

"Moved? By whom?"

"There's an ancient Jewish practice, called ossilegium. In Hebrew, the term is liqqut asamot, which literally means 'bone-gathering.' There are many circumstances in Talmudic literature where remains were relocated for various reasons. In the case of the Jesus Tomb, it was requested by Jewish leaders consulted on the excavation to have the remains from the ossuaries reburied, just outside of Jerusalem."

"Were they put in another ossuary?"

"No," said Damian, "as is traditional, they were all placed in an unmarked collective grave."

"But that seems insane," said Nica, "to let such potentially valuable human remains be put in some random hole in the ground, lost forever."

"Insane to you, maybe, but consider the sacredness of how remains are handled in the Jewish tradition. And this was no random hole. This reburial was according to Jewish law. It was really the only way to keep from creating a public relations nightmare, right in the heart of Israel."

"So then, if no one knows where the remains are buried, and if Hamadi can't get his hands on samples from the ossuaries at the I.A.A., then the whole experiment reaches a dead end?"

"Only if no one knew where the bones were buried," said Damian.

"Someone had to move and rebury the remains in the first place. Did he end up finding a match?"

"He was able to find enough intact nuclear DNA in the bone sample to not only match it to the blood found on the titulus, but he also was able, with the assistance of certain private genetics researchers, to amplify the genome to the point that he could actually do something with it."

"VitaGen," whispered Nica.

"VitaGen indeed. They have been playing with genome amplification since the day they were founded, and they are even involved in..."

"Somatic cell nuclear transfers," said Nica. Her eyes widened and she rested her elbows on the table, her head heavily leaning on her cupped hands. "So this megalomaniacal trust fund baby from Egypt took the genetic code from what he believes were the remains of Jesus Christ and..."

"That's why I'm here," said Damian. "That's why I'm risking my life talking to you. Somewhere out there, at least in theory, is a young man walking around who is carrying Jesus' genetic code in every cell of his body."

9

Elena and Jacob took the bus to a stop around the corner from the Ambassador Hotel. The lobby of the Ambassador was classically inspired, with huge Doric columns buttressing high entryways, replicas of ancient figures dotting the expansive foyer. Jacob was grateful they had upgraded to slacks and button-up shirts. If they had tried to pass in their shorts and T-shirts, the subterfuge likely would have been foiled before they reached the elevator.

"This is a friggin' palace," whispered Jacob as they neared the front desk.

"Welcome to how the other half lives," said Elena.

"Hi," said Jacob. "We have a delivery for Mr. Haman Miller."

The concierge tapped a few keys on his computer, nodding slightly as he pulled up the proper information.

"Yes," said the man, "he's a guest with us." He slid a piece of paper and pen across the desk toward them. "Sign here and we'll have it sent up to his room."

"Sorry," interjected Elena, "but store policy says we have to deliver the clothes to the customer directly. I know it's a dumb rule, but I guess we've had too many complaints about items not making it."

"I assure you," said the concierge, "we don't lose our guests' belongings. It's completely safe with me."

"Oh, I'm sure it is," said Elena, "but here's the thing. We get paid minimum wage in this job, and believe it or not, we have to use our own cars and pay for our own gas to make deliveries. Without tips, we lose money after a whole day of running across town."

"If you live on tips," said the concierge, "why would they send two of you to deliver one suit?"

"We're headed back to the store from a big drop-off," said Jacob.

The concierge let down his professional guard for a moment.

"Miller's up in twelve-thirty-six. Go on up, but be quick, and you didn't get that from me."

"Thanks, brother," said Jacob.

The concierge pressed his fist to his chest in a gesture of solidarity. "Don't let the Man get you down," he said.

* * *

Elena pressed her ear to the hotel room door, putting her finger up to her lips as she glanced at Jacob. After a few moments, she nodded, indicating that someone was inside. Jacob's cheeks tingled as Elena strained to hear the muffled activity on the other side of the solid wood door. After more than a minute of eavesdropping, she stood up and peered in through the peephole in the middle of the door. "I can't see any movement inside," she said, "but it's hard to make anything out, looking through this thing backwards. I think he's in the bathroom. Sounds like the shower just came on."

"All right," whispered Jacob, glancing anxiously over his

shoulder. "So now what?"

"So now we go inside and try to figure out who he is."

"God," groaned Jacob, "that's what I was afraid you were gonna say."

"What the hell did you think we were here for?" said Elena. "To bring him his fucking suit?" She shoved a thin slip of plastic along the seam of the door until she found the bolt. "Good," she said as she jiggled the plastic, "he didn't throw the security lock."

"Does that really work?"

"Not on a deadbolt lock, no," she said, jimmying the card back and forth, "and if this hotel had those updated key card systems, we'd be screwed, too."

Elena bent the card toward the handle and, after pressing downward at a sharp angle, there was a click, followed by the door easing slightly open. She looked over her shoulder and, winking at Jacob, slipped through the crack and into the room.

Elena went immediately to a black satchel sitting on the desk, squinting to see its contents in the dim light. She pulled out a handful of papers along with a Bible, airline tickets, and a map of Denver. She pointed toward the drawer in the nightstand next to the bed and Jacob opened it gingerly, stooping over the opening to get a closer look. As he did, the phone rang next to his head, causing him to leap back in a panic, falling over himself in a tangle on the floor. He looked up at Elena, who was already bending to lift him from the carpet, just as the water in the bathroom shut off.

* * *

Haman reached for the faucet, craning his neck toward the bedroom. Grasping around the curtain for a towel, he wrapped it quickly around himself and stepped out of the tub. The red light next to the receiver blinked as it rang a third time, and Haman reached for it before it could sound again.

"Miller here," he said. He sat on the edge of the bed, running his fingers through the rough stubble along the back of his head. "Yes, thank you for finally calling me back." He reached for a pad of paper and a pen next to the phone. "I think it's time for us to meet in person," he said. "The Bishop has some concerns he would like for me to convey." Haman tapped the end of the pen against the paper. "Well," he said after a pause, "I suggest you make time. We can meet there at your office. Let's say this afternoon, in about an hour."

He hung up the phone without waiting for an answer and stood after scribbling a note to himself. He scanned the room, reached for the closet door and then paused, turning back toward the center of the room as if summoned by an unseen visitor. Finding no one, he turned back toward the closet and opened the door, finding nothing. He walked across to the pair of black pants draped over the desk chair, rifling through the pockets for a slip of paper that wasn't there.

Grumbling incomprehensibly, he returned to the restroom. As he sifted through the contents on the counter for his missing receipt, he heard a thud in the front of his room. He flung the bathroom door wide, revealing a wide column of light dividing the room from the front door.

Haman spun around the corner into the open doorway just as two figures at the other end of the hallway slipped into an open elevator. He started to run after them, his towel slipping from its place around his narrow waist. Grasping at the unraveling knot, he glared venomously toward the space the figures had occupied. Eyes still trained on the elevators, he turned back toward his room, finally lowering his head in frustration, slamming his room door closed.

Hands trembling with rage, he dialed the extension for the front desk. "Hello," he said to the attendant, "this is Haman Miller in twelve-thirty-six. My room has just been robbed. I believe the two perpetrators are still in the hotel. If you see anyone suspicious, stop them. Oh, and don't call the police. I'll be down momentarily to deal with them myself."

★ ★ ★

"Holy shit," gasped Jacob, leaning weakly against the back wall of the elevator as they descended. "I think he saw us."

"If he did," said Elena, "that means they'll probably be expecting us in the lobby." She reached toward the panel and pressed the button for the second floor.

"So what the hell are we gonna do?"

"Fire exit if we have to," said Elena. "We'll get off one floor up and try to make our way out the back."

"But won't that set off an alarm?"

"If there's another way," she said, "we'll take it. But there's no sense in worrying about drawing attention to ourselves at this point. All we can do now is hope we stay a step ahead of him till we get out onto the street."

"Well, we can't go back to our place now," said Jacob breathlessly. "He'll be expecting us there."

"What about Scratch?" Elena asked. "Couldn't we stay with him for a while until we figure out what to do next?"

"Maybe," said Jacob, "but I don't really wanna go there if we can help it. We'll go see Gus."

"Who?"

"Gus," repeated Jacob. "He owns the record store where I work. He'll help us out."

The elevator doors opened on the second floor mezzanine. Elena peeked over the balcony and saw several uniformed men gathering near the front door. She motioned to Jacob to head toward a stairwell in the corner. The two fugitives leapt down the stairs, two and three at a time, until they reached a glass door feeding them onto a sidewalk along the west side of the hotel. Half a block to the right, a city bus was just closing its doors. With a shout, Jacob sprinted toward the lumbering vehicle as it began to pull sleepily away from the curb.

Jacob caught up to the bus as it gathered speed and pounded desperately on the side panel. A passenger at the rear glanced out the window at the scene below, and then called to the driver at the front. The red taillights lit up and the massive wheels slowly ground to a halt. Cars honked angrily from behind them as the bus doors toward the rear opened to invite them in.

* * *

Haman Miller seethed quietly as the elevator numbers ticked down to the lobby. He walked past the uniformed men fanned out now across the lobby, and straight toward the concierge desk.

"You," he growled to the man behind the counter, "take me to your supervisor."

"Sir," said the man, "if there's something I can help you with…"

"Are you the one who let them up to my room?"

73

"Mister Miller?" said the concierge, his voice wavering. "I did send two people from your dry cleaner's up with a delivery, but I had no idea..."

"Take me to your supervisor now." The man cowered under Haman's piercing glare.

"I'd be happy to call him to the front if you'd like." The concierge gulped.

"If you don't take me to your supervisor's office in five seconds," said Haman, "I'll spread the back of your skull across that wall behind you. Five...four...three..."

"Right," nodded the man frantically. "This way, please." He led Haman behind the counter and down a narrow, windowless hallway, washed of all of its life by rows of fluorescent bulbs. As the door to the front desk closed behind them, Haman shoved his forearm across the man's shoulders, pinning him against the wall. Helplessly squirming, he strained to look behind him, without success.

"Who were they?" said Haman, steady and cold in his tone.

"Who?" gasped the concierge. "The dry cleaning people?" As he spoke, he felt the unforgiving pressure of the barrel of a gun against the base of his skull, followed by the click-click of a bullet settling into the chamber.

"I'll ask you one more time," said Haman. "If you don't give me a satisfactory answer, it will be the last mistake you ever make. Now, who were they?" The young man began to whimper, his arms falling slack to his sides. Haman pressed harder against the back of the concierge's head.

"There were two of them," he whined, tears seeping from the corners of his eyes. "Please, God, don't kill me."

"Keep going," said Haman, leaning his full weight against the young man's back. He could smell the sourness of Haman's breath as he hissed in his ear.

"One girl and one guy, maybe twenty years old."

"And?"

"And the guy was, I don't know, Hispanic, or maybe Arabic. The girl was white. They said they had to deliver a suit to your room."

"And you let them," said Haman.

"Please, man," said the concierge. "I told you everything. I screwed up, and I'm really, really sorry. I have a wife and a baby. I'll do whatever you want. Just please don't shoot me." Haman lowered the gun and stepped back from the young man, who promptly fell into a sobbing heap on the floor. The concierge held his face in his hands as he continued to plead for his life, but when he looked up, his assailant was gone.

10

When Jacob and Elena arrived at Revolution Records, Gus was rifling through a pile of albums someone had dropped off after an estate sale. "I don't know who's more ignorant," he said, plucking an old Led Zeppelin cover from the stack, "the people who miss this stuff at yard sales, or the ones who bring their leftovers to me. I gave this lady fifty bucks for this whole box, and look at one of the first things I found in here."

"Zeppelin," said Jacob. "So?"

"So," grunted Gus. "Do you see the turquoise lettering, here in the corner?" He pointed at the band name at the top left, and then the record label logo in the opposite corner, both in light blue against the black and white image of a flaming dirigible. "That makes this record worth a shitload of money. In this condition, I can probably get a grand for it on eBay. More from my collectors in Europe."

"Did you know that was in there when you offered her fifty dollars?" asked Jacob.

"Hey, I just make them an offer," he said. "They don't have to take it if they don't want to. This lady's husband probably died. She's probably just glad to get them out of her house."

"Lucky for you, I guess," said Jacob, slouching over the

counter. The sound of Charlie Parker's tune, "Billie's Bounce," drifted down on them.

"Who's your friend?"

"Yeah, this is Elena," Jacob said. "Elena, this is my boss, Gus."

"Pleasure," said Gus. "I guess if you hang around this guy, you must be into jazz."

"Sorta, yeah," she said. "I mean, I didn't know a whole lot about it before I met Jacob. But I like what he's shown me."

Gus smiled.

"I bet," said Gus. "So why the hell are you here? You don't work today."

"Well, today has been pretty fucked up," said Jacob. "I woke up this morning and someone was robbing my room."

"No shit," said Gus. "With you in it?"

"Not exactly," said Jacob, his face turning slightly red.

"Ahh," nodded Gus. "Right on."

"Anyway," said Jacob, "this guy took off when he heard me coming, but we tracked him down to this hotel downtown."

"The Ambassador," said Elena.

"Why the hell would some guy who could afford to stay at the Ambassador be interested in taking anything you have?" asked Gus.

"I still don't know," said Jacob. "He trashed my room, but it didn't look like he actually stole anything."

"So he didn't mess with your horn?"

"Shit," Jacob rolled his eyes. "I forgot it."

"So just go back and get it," said Gus.

"That's the thing," said Jacob. "We kind of broke into his room at the hotel."

"Dude," Gus rubbed his chin, "that's pretty stupid."

"And while we were in there," said Jacob, "he came out of the bathroom."

"You busted in while the guy was in his room?" Gus said. "You have bigger balls than I gave you credit for. That, or you have a death wish."

"He came after us," said Elena, "but we got away and came here."

"Did he follow you?"

"Don't think so," said Jacob.

"If you led some whack job to my place," said Gus, "I'm gonna kick your narrow butt." Jacob grabbed the phone from across the counter, handing it to Elena.

"Would you do me a favor and call Allen," he said. "Ask him to bring my horn down here?" Elena nodded and wandered toward the front of the store as she dialed.

"Look," said Jacob, turning back toward Gus, "I didn't mean to, but I got this girl I really like involved in something that I'm worried could be dangerous."

"Okay," said Gus, "so none of that explains why you came here."

"We can't go back home right now," Jacob said. "It's just too risky. He knows where we live, I mean he must since he broke in, right? I was kind of hoping that we could crash with you for a while."

"With me?" said Gus. "I don't think so."

"Come on," said Jacob.

"All right," Gus said. "But don't expect anything other than some horizontal space."

★ ★ ★

The walls of the apartment were exposed brick, stretching twelve feet high where they met with the exposed vent work and galvanized wiring ducts that snaked through the space. The oversized windows, tinted a pale green hue like that of old soft drink bottles, looked out over both the Denver skyline and the Rocky Mountains in the distance.

"Wow," said Elena, peering out one of the three picture windows. "This is one sweet place you've got."

"Seriously," said Jacob.

"I like the view," Gus said, settling into the couch. "Helps me relax."

"Hey, we really appreciate this, Gus," Jacob said, leaning against the counter. "Letting us crash your sanctuary and all."

"Sure. Just don't mess up my stuff, and don't get too used to the view."

"You're the best," Elena said.

"Whatever," Gus said, turning toward the door. "Just a few days, right?"

Jacob nodded and Gus closed the door behind him.

* * *

"Usually," said Scratch, "I'm happy if you show up for our weekly meetings. Seeing you twice in just a few days is a special treat." He rubbed the contour of his jaw line with the tips of his fingers. "By the way, I wanted to tell you how much I enjoyed your performance on Friday. You really have developed wonderfully as an artist."

"Thanks," Jacob said, "it's a pretty fun place to play. They're good guys to jam with."

"Lovely lady, too," Scratch grinned. "Elena, wasn't it?"

"Yeah, but don't start giving me shit about it."

"Of course not," said Scratch. "I could tell you really like her."

"It's not like we're getting married or anything," Jacob slumped down in his seat.

"I know, but you like her. So what's up? "

Jacob told Scratch about the break-in, the incident at the hotel, and their subsequent flight to Gus's apartment. After he finished the story, Jacob took a deep breath, shifted nervously in his chair and watched Scratch in silence. The priest nodded, rubbing his index finger back and forth across his upper lip.

"Well, at least you're all right," he said after a long pause. "That's what's most important."

"I just don't really know what to do now."

"Have you fallen behind on any bills, or taken out any—private loans?"

"Dude," said Jacob, "I told you it didn't have anything to do with money. And before you ask, no, I'm not doing drugs. I don't gamble, I'm not a criminal—except for breaking into that guy's hotel room I guess—and I'm not working for the mob. I just go to work, play my horn, go to my gigs, and lately I've been spending some time with Elena. That's about it."

Scratch frowned.

"What?" Jacob sat up. "I know that look."

"I don't know," he said. "I'm just thinking. How long have you known Elena, I mean, before you started seeing each other?"

"She was living at the co-op when I got there. Why?"

"Just curious," said Scratch. "Does she seem overly inquisitive about your background or anything?"

"No, not really," said Jacob. "What, you think she's some kind of narc?" He shook his head. "That's not possible."

"You're probably right."

"She's cool," said Jacob. "I'm sure."

"I assume she has a key to your room?"

"Sure," Jacob shrugged. "She borrows clothes and stuff sometimes."

"How about anyone else?" Scratch said.

"Except for Allen and the people at the front desk of the co-op, no."

"Who is Allen?"

"Just a buddy," said Jacob. "He's totally cool. Harmless as a fly and too perpetually stoned to be involved in anything sinister."

"You don't think he would ever compromise your friendship if he needed money?"

"Shit, no," said Jacob. "He's loaded. When his folks died, they left these huge life insurance policies behind."

"So why would someone break in?"

11

Bodies were strewn along the streets, left as warnings to followers of the one called The Christ. Loved ones were threatened with a similar fate if they dared to bury their dead, so the stench of rotting flesh hung along roadside ditches like a necrotic fog. The loose network of followers collectively began to cower, terrified by the very sight of one another. Some fled to Tarsus or the island of Cypress, while others simply disappeared into the wilderness.

Ya'aqov, wary but undeterred, sent word for his mother and Mariamne, who had helped care for her along with Salome in his absence. Her age prohibited much travel, so they convened at the home of a cousin outside of Jerusalem. Guided by moonlight, Ya'aqov waited until the streets were silent, slipping through the door like a ghost.

He found Maryam and Mariamne waiting there for him, their faces golden in the flickering light of the evening fire.

Maryam sobbed at the sight of her son, her tears falling freely. Mariamne, who also braved the threats upon her life to carry Yeshua's message when she was not with Maryam, threw her arms around Ya'aqov.

"It has been too long," Mariamne smiled, finally releasing him only to arm's-length, where she held him. "You look well."

"I must appear better than I feel, then," Ya'aqov smiled weakly.

"Are you ill?" Maryam placed a hand on her son's cheek.

"Could be nothing more than exhaustion," he said. "I hardly sleep anymore, worrying about the fate I've brought upon our brothers and sisters. As soon as I close my eyes, I see them suffering. I arise, covered in sweat, sure that I have the stain of their blood on my hands."

"You cannot blame yourself for these things that are happening," said Mariamne.

"So much blood, and still more to come," whispered Ya'aqov, holding his head in his hands.

"The words we share are precious, more so even than the lives lost for its sake," said Maryam. She fell silent then spoke quietly. "The guards—the Romans—they're looking for you."

"Imagine that," Ya'aqov said and snorted.

"But Ya'aqov," said Maryam, grasping at his sleeve, "they intend to kill you. There is another way."

"You mean the Essenoi?" said Ya'aqov. "You are suggesting that I skulk off to live in the caves of Qumran like a hermit?"

"Not forever," said Maryam. "You can still be of help in Qumran, and you can take the opportunity to learn from the Brethren."

"Learn what? Yeshua taught me everything I needed to know."

"Yes," said Mariamne, "but where do you think he learned? It's said that he spent some years in Qumran, learning the ways of healing and peace of the Essenoi. Think of how much more you could bring to the cause if you had insight into some of the sources of inspiration for his ministry."

* * *

Before there was enough sunlight to cast a shadow, they were headed toward Qumran. Though rocky, the trail largely led downhill, toward the western bank of the Dead Sea, where the small community lay. It was a long day's walk, but one that pilgrims before them had made, including Ya'aqov's brother, Yeshua.

Mariamne and Ya'aqov walked mostly in silence, broken up only by occasional stops to reaffirm their bearing. With every hour the air grew heavier and thicker with moisture as they descended toward the coastline. By dusk, they spotted the contour of the water's edge in the distance. Tired but encouraged by the sight of their destination, they pushed on until late evening, when they arrived at Qumran.

Ya'aqov was surprised by the size of the community. Where he had expected to find a hundred or so men, there were no more than thirty. What had once served as a fortress for the eastern provinces had been converted into a small pottery factory after the Romans seized control. Only a few feet below the sandy surface, the land was rich with clay, good for plates, jars, and other vessels necessary for preservation.

The silhouettes of the Essenoi danced maniacally as the surrounding torches flickered and shuddered under the cool evening breeze from the sea. An old man in a white robe like some sort of apparition turned his attention to Ya'aqov.

"Brother of Yeshua," the old man said, bowing deeply, eyes closed, "you are welcome here among us. Please, come. Rest."

Ya'aqov bowed, his eyes looking from one robed monk to another. Mariamne placed her hand on the small of his back, ushering him in the direction the old man was walking. A meal of fish, goat cheese, and dates sat on a mat in the middle of what appeared to be a large communal dining area. No one met his eyes. Aside from the old man's hospitality, Ya'aqov felt invisible among the Essenoi.

"Do they speak?" asked Ya'aqov, through a mouthful of cheese.

"Of course," said the old man. "All of them are quite eager to meet you. But our way is to speak only when necessary. My name is Benyamin."

* * *

Ya'aqov awoke the next morning to the droning chant of the Essenoi, invoking the divine to guide the works of the coming day with wisdom, clarity, and peace. He could only understand parts of their prayers, as they used many melodic chants that had no words he could distinguish at all. In unison, the monks raised their hands toward the sky, faces heavenward, and then they prostrated themselves against the dirt. They continued this, apparently oblivious to Ya'aqov's presence, long enough for him to hunt down a drink, secure some flatbread, and find Mariamne in her quarters.

The daylight afforded him much more detail about their surroundings than the night before when they had arrived. The walls of each chamber, built eight to ten to a row, were made of straw and pale brown mud, each reaching only slightly above his waist. The floors were all tamped dirt, and there were a few spaces evidently dedicated to communal living, all of which were open to the air above.

Ya'aqov assumed that the chamber where the monks now were gathered was some sort of rustic chapel. There were no icons or symbols to denote holy ground, and from what he could tell by their behavior as they broke from their worship ritual, there was little hierarchy among them, if any. The only distinguishing characteristics he could find from one to another were the amount and color of facial hair many of them grew in abundance.

Ya'aqov noticed now that a few of the members who he had thought were young men last night from a distance were actually women. Since each bore the same loose-fitting garments as the men, they were hard to distinguish from the younger male members of the order. The monks began to disperse, again without any acknowledgment of their guests beyond a polite bow from Benyamin, with groups of five or six breaking off to perform various tasks.

A few grabbed nets and turned toward the coastline, while others faced in the direction of a nearby grove of trees, baskets tucked beneath their arms. Some grabbed digging tools from a nearby wall and knelt next to a clay pit, and half a dozen men and women approached a limestone cliff face, which was much closer to the monastery than Ya'aqov had realized. Though barefoot, the monks scuttled up the sheer mountainside without hesitation, vanishing into shadowy caves, carved out of the side of the stone at varying heights.

"Those," said Benyamin, appearing next to Ya'aqov, "are our scribes. Some record prophecies or transcribe oral stories, and then others copy what has been recorded." Mariamne rose from her seated position, squinting in the harsh morning light reflecting off of the surrounding rock. Ya'aqov pointed to one of the women in the crew of fishers, smiling bemusedly.

"Look there," he said. "They work their women just as if they were men. Next, you'll show me a man washing the dishes."

"We share all responsibilities," said Benyamin. "We believe in the equality of all people."

Ya'aqov raised his eyebrow warily. "Do you now?" he said. "You'd consider a Roman soldier, one of those pagans who practically reduced this place to rubble, as your equal?" Benyamin bowed his head slightly, smiling. "Ridiculous. And I've never heard of an order like this with men and women living together. It's a wonder there's time for any prayer, what with all the nonsense that must go on after the sun descends."

"We are a people who have avowed a life of chastity," said Benyamin. "There is no consorting."

"Or else what?"

"There simply isn't," said Benyamin. "It's not an issue. We have no punitive consequences, as we have no formal leadership. Everything is governed by consensus. Some have gifts of one sort or another, but no individual is valued any more than another." Ya'aqov rolled his eyes at Mariamne, who scowled at him.

"You're an odd lot," said Ya'aqov, shaking his head.

"Yeshua said you were the passionate but skeptical type," said Benyamin. "In time, you will better understand our ways. In the meantime, please feel free to orient yourself. Anyone here will be happy to answer any question you may have." The old man bowed deeply and turned toward the limestone cliffs. He leapt from one outcropping to another like a man half his age.

"Crazy codger," Ya'aqov said, kicking the brick wall next to him.

"The Essenoi are gracious people," said Mariamne. "They have welcomed me just as warmly, every time over the years."

"Over the years?" Jacob said and turned to face her. "You've been here before?"

"I visited Yeshua here several times," she said. "He learned much from them, and they from him."

"So all of those years," said Ya'aqov, "when Mother thought he was either dead or traveling the world, he was really right here, within a day's walk."

"Not all of the time."

"He could have told us," Ya'aqov said. "He didn't have to hide out here in the wilderness."

"And what parent would allow a boy of twelve to live in a place like this?"

12

"What the hell's the matter with you?" Edward said, munching on a handful of sunflower seeds.

"It's this guy I talked to at lunch," Nica said, sitting on the corner of his desk.

"Tell me where he lives," said Edward. "He's as good as dead."

"No, nothing like that," she said. "He's cute, but this was business."

"Oh, was this the dead guy?" Nica nodded. "No wonder you look weird. I'd be off-center too if I had lunch with a cute corpse."

"He told me more about this story I'm tracking down about the titulus crucis. It's a lot bigger than I thought."

"Let me guess," said Edward, "you want more travel money."

"Not yet," said Nica, "but I might soon." She recounted to Edward what Damian Armitage had shared with her. By the time she finished, his mouth hung open slightly. "You have a seed stuck to your bottom lip," she said.

"That's some messed up story," he said, "but unless you can prove it's true, it's not exactly New Yorker material. Leads from a dead guy, some mysterious Egyptian Svengali, and a clone of Jesus walking around the planet...sounds like something for your tabloid friends."

"I'm not making this shit up, Edward."

"I believe you," he said, "but you're not going to Egypt. Forget it."

"I know."

"Or Germany. No way."

Nica rifled through her notes and entered the number for the Max Planck Institute.

"Hallo," said the voice on the other end of the line.

"Dr. Pavel," said Nica, grabbing a pen, "this is Miss Di Seta from the New Yorker."

"Miss Di Seta," said Dr. Pavel, "I did not expect to be speaking again so soon."

"I've had some developments on my end I'd like to discuss with you. I wonder if you have a moment?"

"Actually," said Dr. Pavel, "I was on my way out for the evening, but what may I do for you?"

"Well," said Nica, taking a breath, "there have been some interesting developments related to the matters we discussed before. I believe I understand the nature of your research with the titulus a little better now. It's my hope that we might be able to help one another."

"I don't see how a journalist can benefit my research."

"I know you're being watched," said Nica. "I think I might be able to move a little more freely to gather data that might be of great assistance to you. However, I can't do that unless I know where to look."

"Miss Di Seta," said Dr. Pavel, "you're speaking in generalities I don't understand."

"I spoke with Damian Armitage today," said Nica. "I understand about the samples taken from the sites outside of Jeru-

90

salem nearly twenty years ago, and the work of an Egyptian named Hamadi Chamoun. I understand the implication of his work, as well as your resistance to acknowledge the existence of The Project. I sympathize with your concern for your own welfare and that of your family, but I hope we can both agree to be honest with one another."

"How is it that I may help you?" said Dr. Pavel. The warmth had drained from his voice.

"I believe there's a young man walking around somewhere in whom you have great interest. If you thought you could get to him yourself, you would have done it by now. But because you are taking the threats you've received seriously, you're not sure you'd ever get that far."

"And?"

"And I can get to him," said Nica. "If I know who I'm looking for." She paused. "You know who it is I'm looking for, don't you, Dr. Pavel?"

There was no answer for a moment. Finally, she heard a sigh.

"I suppose I was not entirely honest with you the last time we spoke," he said. "For that, I apologize. However, this is a much more involved situation than I had anticipated, and the last thing I want to do is drag someone else into a dangerous situation."

"You haven't dragged me into anything," said Nica. "It's my choice to keep pushing this issue, and if I can't get what I need from you, I'm afraid I'll have to find some other way. But I expect we can make one another's lives a little easier."

"I suppose you're right," said Dr. Pavel.

"What do you need?" Nica asked. "Blood? Are you hoping to find a sample from the young man who was the subject of this experiment?"

"If I had such a sample," he said, "it could prove quite compelling, for both of our purposes, I expect."

"Tell me where to go. I'll find him."

"There's a woman," said Dr. Pavel, "who lives in Colorado. Her name is Colette Harrigan. I have tried without success to contact her from a distance. I'm afraid if I traveled abroad to find her myself, I would put her life, among others, in danger. But you may still have some time to find her and try to earn her trust."

"A woman," said Nica, "I thought it was a kid we were looking for—a young man?"

"Ultimately," said Pavel. "But if we have any chance of finding him, your best avenue is by speaking with this woman."

"So who is she?"

"In 1988, she was nineteen years old, living with friends, barely making ends meet. She agreed to serve as a surrogate mother for a local organization in Denver. Though there is record of her receiving a one-time payment of five thousand dollars for her involvement, there is no trace of the child she supposedly bore, or who raised it."

"How in the hell would you learn all of this from Germany?" Nica asked.

"The agency went bankrupt several years later," he said. "Their records were stored at a local hospital where the mothers and children received their medical care. As a doctor, I was able to call up their records office and have them search through the file for me."

* * *

Nica booked the last flight out to Denver that night, making a stop along the way at her apartment to pick up some clothes. When she opened her door, there was an unmarked envelope on the floor. "Shit," she whispered, studying the outside of the plain white package. It was a note from Damian Armitage:

Dear Nica,

I'm sure by now that you are on your way to finding what you're looking for. It was with some ambivalence that I came to you in the first place, as I am concerned that the information I have shared with you, if not my very presence, would put you in harm's way. Had I not felt that you would pursue this on your own without my help, we likely would have never met.

I was grateful for our brief time together. It is rare that I have the chance any more to enjoy a meal with someone so intelligent, let alone so lovely. It is my hope that we will have an opportunity, under better circumstances, to meet again and continue where we left off.

With warmest regards,
Damian

* * *

The Denver air was crisp and dry, causing the skin of Nica's face to tighten. Nica grabbed a sweater out of her bag and hopped into her rental car to head into town. Edward had recommended the Ambassador hotel. Her room was located on the ninth floor. She opened the drapes wide, standing inches from the oversized window. Looking down caused her head to spin a little.

The address Nica had found for Colette Harrigan took her

to an apartment complex in Golden, about twenty miles west of Denver in the foothills of the Rocky Mountains. The community was made up largely of commuters who couldn't afford to live either in Boulder to the north or in Denver, as well as municipal workers, off-season ski resort employees, and staff members at the local brewery. Colette's complex sat on a mesa overlooking the rest of the valley, where the historic portion of Golden lay.

The complex was oddly named The Oasis, surrounded on all sides by prairie grass, piñon trees, a smattering of evergreens, and rugged outcroppings of dark volcanic rock. The paneling on the units was painted a seemingly random combination of aquamarine, peach, pale yellow, and pistachio.

Nica searched the numbers on each apartment door, painted on the breast of a colorful parrot, for the one that would lead her to Colette. The woman who answered the door was stooped and shallow-chested. She clenched in her teeth a cigarette with an astonishingly long ash dangling from the end. She squinted into the daylight at Nica.

"Can I help you?" said the woman.

"I'm looking for Colette Harrigan."

"Yeah," the woman stared blankly back at her. Nica extended her hand to the woman, who examined it before offering her own.

"My name is Nica," she said, pulling a card from her purse with her free hand. "I'm with the New Yorker magazine. I wonder if I could ask you a few questions."

"New York," said the woman, taking a drag from her cigarette. "You're a long way from home."

"Actually, I came all the way here to see you."

"You did, huh?"

"Colette, may I buy you some breakfast, or at least a coffee?"

"Don't drink coffee," the woman said. She looked over her shoulder at the dingy surroundings of her apartment, then glanced back at Nica. "Guess I could go for some breakfast though."

* * *

Colette eyed the taps behind the bar before returning to her menu. Nica walked over to a table. The place was a bar that made a little extra by serving breakfast and lunch. They were the only people there besides the waitress.

"Still a little too early for a drink," Colette said.

"Order whatever you like," said Nica. "On me, of course. I appreciate you taking the time."

They sat.

"So what's this about?" said Colette once her order of scrambled eggs and ham steak arrived.

"I'm working on a story that might have something to do with when you were younger," Nica said.

Colette snorted.

"That was a different lifetime, but go ahead."

"Have you lived here your whole life?"

"Grew up in Greeley, a ranching town northeast of here," said Colette. "Worked cattle with my dad until I finished school, then I moved to Denver to try going out on my own."

"From the farm to the big city," said Nica.

"Got tired of the smell of cow shit," Colette said.

"Are you married?" Nica said, and took a sip from her cup. Colette shook her head. "Any kids?" Colette narrowed her eyes.

"Remind me what this story is about that you're writing."

"Sorry," Nica leaned back in her chair. "I know, I'm getting ahead of myself. We're interested in doing a piece about a family planning organization that used to be located in Denver called Little Angels. You're familiar with it?"

"I know it," said Colette.

"Well, mostly they handled adoptions and such, but they also did some work with surrogates. They went out of business several years ago, but we have reason to believe they were involved in some unusual practices. I'm hopeful that you'll be able to fill in some blanks for me. In return, I might be able to provide you with some information, if you want it, of course."

"Information?"

"About your son," said Nica. The waitress brought more coffee, but Colette's gaze didn't waver.

"I don't know what you're talking about," she said. "You got the wrong person."

"I understand this is all personal, and of course you'd never be mentioned in the story. I'm just looking for information."

"Who the hell are you?" Colette asked.

"I'm a reporter," said Nica, "but I also know what it's like to lose a baby." Colette stared at Nica, who smiled warmly.

13

Elena looked up from reading a Variety magazine on the couch when Jacob opened Gus's front door. She was sitting cross-legged, wearing nothing but an oversized T-shirt. "How'd you get back so fast?" she said. "Did he stand you up?"

"Actually, Scratch paid for a cab to bring me back," said Jacob.

"That was nice. So now we have a couple of hours before we have to meet Allen. What do you want to do?"

"We could grab something to eat," he said, "but first I need to hop in the shower."

* * *

The water was soothing, and Jacob noticed that it was hotter than what he was used to. He had to turn the temperature down three times. As he rinsed the lather from his hair, he noticed a reddish-brown tint to the water swirling down the drain.

"Fuck me!" shouted Jacob, lowering his arms to inspect his wrists. They were seeping blood again.

"What's that?" Elena called from the living room.

"Nothing," he called out. "Dropped the soap."

Jacob sat in the tub, pressing his arms across one another

against his chest. He closed his eyes and tried to slow his breathing. When he looked back down at his arms, the bleeding had stopped.

"Mind if I put on some music?" asked Elena.

The rich layered tones of Andrew Hill's album Dusk mingled with the sound of the shower.

What a choice, thought Jacob. Dusk was inspired by Karintha, a principal character from Cane, a book by the Harlem Renaissance writer Jean Toomer. Karintha, like Elena, was a young woman forced to grow up fast. The first notes from Hill's tune evoked Jacob's favorite lines from the book:

> Her skin is like dusk on the eastern horizon
> When the sun goes down.

"You better not be jerking off in there," called Elena.

"Almost done," he said, rinsing the remaining blood from the tub.

★ ★ ★

"Poor baby," Elena said softly. "When did this happen again? Why didn't you tell me?"

"In the shower."

"Does it hurt?" she asked, running her fingers gently over the marks. Jacob shook his head.

"Freaked me out though," he said. "Before, it was always at night."

Elena rested her head against Jacob's chest, her ear pressed against his heart. She stroked his stomach with the palm of her hand and Jacob, eyes closed, rested his head on the back of the couch.

"I need to show you something," Elena said. She took his hand and ran it along the inside of her arm. For the first time, he noticed a faint pink raised line running laterally from her wrist up toward her elbow. Both sides of the scar were punctuated by several small suture marks. There was a similar scar on the inside of her other arm.

"God," said Jacob. "How old were you?"

"Thirteen," she said. "My dad was being a total dick all the time. Never could keep his hands to himself. I had no idea what to—"

"Did he rape you?"

"No," said Elena. "It was fucked up, the stuff he tried, but I think he was too scared to actually do that. He did just enough to keep me plenty ashamed of myself."

"So you tried to kill yourself."

"Sorta," she said. "I did it about ten minutes before he got home, right out where he'd find me. I wanted to find some way to punish him."

"That's really sad," said Jacob, stroking the back of her neck. "I'm sorry."

"Typical fucked up parent stuff," she said.

"Makes me almost glad I didn't know my parents."

"You're probably descended from royalty or something," Elena said, kissing him on the chin.

"Right," said Jacob, "the kind of royalty that dumps their kid at an orphanage."

* * *

Jacob and Elena washed their New York slices down with soft drinks while sitting on the curb. Allen was late. So they ordered another slice each. They sat across from the club. Jacob had tried the door but it was still locked. Everyone else was late as usual.

"I remember how freaked out I was the first time I played in front of people," said Jacob, taking a sip from his drink. "I was about fourteen and I played a solo at mass. Scratch wanted me to play 'Amazing Grace,' which I already knew by heart, but when I got up there to play, I was so nervous I could hardly make enough spit to get the sound to come out."

"It's hard to imagine you nervous," said Elena. "You look so confident up there, almost like you're in a different place."

"I feel that way now," Jacob said, "but there was a time when I was more worried about what other people thought of my playing than I did about the music I was making. Then I just felt like a freak or something."

The club door opened and a few members of the band walked in. Jacob and Elena finished their slices and crossed the street.

"It must be nice," Elena said, watching as the drummer hauled his stuff through the door and tripped over his bag of cymbals, "to have something you can just disappear into, any time you want."

"Can't afford a plane ticket," he said, "so I guess I use music instead."

Allen shuffled through the door with bags on both of his shoulders and Jacob's saxophone case in his hand. He collapsed into an empty chair, gasping. "I need a fucking cigarette," he groaned.

"You're so out of shape, it's pathetic," Elena said, picking up her bag from the floor.

"That Celia," said Allen, tucking his hair behind his ears, "is a class-A ball-busting bitch."

"Why?" asked Jacob. "What did she do?"

"Gave me a hard time about walking out with your stuff," he said. "I told her you asked me to, but no matter what I said, she wouldn't believe me. Finally, I told her to kiss my ass and I walked out anyway. She bitched at me from the door of the co-op for almost a block."

"Was she asking a lot of questions?" Elena said.

"Yeah, she wanted to know where you guys had gone to, where you were staying, when you were coming back. You know, standard ball-buster shit." Elena looked anxiously at Jacob, then back at Allen.

"And what did you tell her?"

"What do you think?" said Allen. "I told her to fuck off."

"Thanks for dealing with her," said Jacob. "Order whatever you want. It's on us."

"Unless you've got some weed," sighed Allen, "I can take care of myself."

* * *

Jacob woke the next morning on the couch with Elena's feet next to his head. His movement caused her to stir, and she waved at him with her feet. "Hey down there," she said, stretching her arms above her head. "That was awesome last night."

"Yeah," Jacob pushed himself up to his elbows, "it was a little rough on the couch, but when you're motivated..."

"If you guys are going to copulate on my couch again," came a voice from the bedroom, "please put down a towel or something. That couch is dry clean only."

Elena giggled, her bare breast slipping out from beneath the blanket they were sharing. Jacob gave his end a playful tug, exposing her to the waist.

"Sorry, Gus," said Jacob, reaching for his boxers on the floor.

"It'd be better if you guys would put my records back when you're done listening to them. That Iggy Pop album is worth seventy-five bucks, you know."

"Would you eat some breakfast if I made something?" Elena asked.

"Nah," said Gus. "I can't eat anything besides fruit in the morning."

Elena held the blanket to her chest with one hand and pulled her T-shirt over to her with the other. She felt along the floor with her foot until she snagged her panties with her toes. Then Elena stopped mid-stretch and stared at her arm.

"What the hell?!" Elena exclaimed.

"You alright?" Jacob said from the living room.

He walked into the bathroom to find her sitting on the toilet, staring at her arms.

"Look," Elena said, extending her arms toward him. Jacob took her slender forearm in his hand, inspecting the pale underside.

"What?" said Jacob.

"My scars are gone!"

14

Ya'aqov strolled along the coastline, kicking pebbles into the water. As the sun rose in the cloudless sky, Ya'aqov came upon several of the monks who were casting nets from a skiff just off the shore. He sat on a rock to watch. Their movements, combined with the warmth of the sun, had an entrancing effect. Ya'aqov did not realize he had closed his eyes until a figure came between him and the sunlight.

"Good morning," said Benyamin.

Ya'aqov squinted toward the shadowy figure standing over him. Benyamin lowered himself to a seated position, facing Ya'aqov. "How are you finding your new home?"

"Strangely comfortable. It's nice not to have to look over my shoulder."

The two walked silently down the shore, Ya'akov's jaw muscles clenching and relaxing as he ground his teeth together. "So," he finally said, glancing over at Benyamin. "Tell me of your time with Yeshua."

"He was a young man," said Benyamin. "He came to us seeking wisdom and guidance. We offered what we could, but I'm afraid he nourished us more than we helped him."

"How long was he here?"

"Two years, maybe more. We don't follow a calendar as

such. But while he was with us, he must have grown at least two hands in height."

"What was he seeking?" asked Ya'aqov.

"Fullness."

"Fullness," said Ya'aqov, "of what?"

"Fullness of being."

"You're as vague as he was," Ya'aqov said, stomping on a broken, weathered branch.

"Life is rather different here," said Benyamin. "In time, you will become more familiar."

"I feel like a fugitive," Ya'aqov scowled. "A coward."

"Part of accepting fullness of being is abstinence from force. In some cases, this may be physical force, and in others it may have to do more with patience. You will know when it is time for you to return to Jerusalem, if the time doesn't place you there first."

"Do you always speak in such abstract expressions?"

"Ya'aqov, consider the possibility that, though you have found yourself devoted to the message Yeshua brought to the world, it was not him you were following, but rather the call of your own heart."

"You know," said Ya'aqov, "for an old man who says he's committed to a life of silence, you have a great deal to say."

Benyamin smiled.

★ ★ ★

"I thought you said you wrote on scrolls," said Ya'aqov, running his fingers gently over the intricate symbols set in relief on the book cover. They were standing at a large crudely made wooden table inside a cave.

"Oh, we did not write this," said Benyamin. "This comes from the court of King Solomon himself." Ya'aqov opened the cover slowly. On the inside, inscribed in immaculate Hebrew characters, were the words The Sacred Book of Remedies.

"What's this?" said Ya'aqov. "Some kind of healing book?"

"Fifty generations or more ago," said Benyamin, "this book was written by Solomon and the wisest of his spiritual counsel. It has been handed on from generation to generation since the end of his reign. We consider this to be the most sacred text we possess. Some would sacrifice many lives to acquire it, but in the wrong hands, its power would be subject to great abuse."

"So why show it to me?" asked Ya'aqov. "Why even trust me?"

"Brother of Yeshua, you have many questions. Begin here. Come with me again tomorrow and we will study these writings together. If you want to know more about the brother whom you so dearly loved, many of your answers may be contained here."

15

"When I was in college," said Nica, "I dated a few guys. Nobody serious, but I did my share of exploring. I went out with this one guy for about three weeks, and I really started to like him. He said all the right things, and he was charming, plus it didn't hurt that he was from a rich family."

"I could go for that," said Colette, sopping a piece of her biscuit in a pool of gravy.

"Right," nodded Nica. "I mean, what young girl wouldn't have a thing for a guy like that, right? Anyway, one thing led to another, and we had a little too much to drink this one night. Up to then I hadn't slept with him, and I was actually starting to get a reputation on campus as a prude."

"You, a prude?" said Colette. "I can't imagine that. You must have had guys trying to get in bed with you all the time."

"Thanks. But see, I had the good old Catholic guilt working for me. I was a virgin until after high school." Colette's eyes widened. She stuffed another biscuit in her mouth. "That was the thing," Nica went on. "I should have known better. He was just a little too smooth, and I was a little too drunk."

"Wait," said Colette, "you mean this guy is the one who…"

"Took my virginity?"

"I wasn't gonna put it that nice, but yeah."

"So against my better judgment I agreed to go up to his place after dinner, and one thing led to another. Next thing I knew, I missed my next period. I was so naïve, I still didn't know what was going on."

"How could you not know if you're pregnant?"

"Equal parts ignorance and denial," said Nica. "I went along for a couple more weeks like nothing was different, until a friend of mine bought a test for me. Of course, it came up positive, and I nearly lost my mind."

"Getting pregnant isn't the end of the world," said Colette.

"For my mother, it would have been."

"So you didn't tell her?"

"No way," Nica shook her head. "Not only would she have yanked me out of school, but she would have probably sent me to live in a convent. Finally, I decided to tell this guy— Robert was his name—and he just sat there and stared at me, like I was speaking another language. I expected him at least to freak out, yell at me, blame me for it or something, but he just stared at me, with no change in his expression."

"That prick."

"Yeah, well, I learned something about men that day," said Nica. "It was the last time I ever saw Robert, at least as a lover. I'd see him around town and he'd wave like we were old acquaintances, but we never said another word to each other again."

"So what did you do?"

"The only thing I thought I could do," said Nica. "I went down to this clinic where some other girls I knew had gone and I had it taken care of." Colette looked down at her plate, stirring the gravy in nervous circles. "My friend who took me, the same one who bought the pregnancy test, kept telling me that it was for the best, and that I didn't want to throw my life away over some stupid, drunken mistake. But afterwards, I just felt for the longest time like something was missing.

"After that, I pretty much wrote off men all together and focused all of my energy on school. I didn't date. I hardly even went out. I had a couple of friends, but mostly I just kept to myself."

"That's real sad," said Colette. "I'm sorry that happened to you."

"Well," said Nica, "the way I look at it, that was the moment when my naïveté about how I thought the world worked vanished." Nica snapped her fingers. "Gone, just like that. It's not the world's fault, but it definitely put things in a different light for me."

"So do you have any kids now?" asked Colette. Nica shook her head.

"I date here and there, mostly when friends set me up, but something in me just won't let me take the risk. So it never ends up working out really." Colette nodded solemnly. "How about you," said Nica, "any children?"

"Two," said Colette. "Boy and a girl. Adam is seven and Sophie is three. Two different dads, neither one is around. I have about as high of an opinion of men as you do."

"We know how to pick them, don't we?" Nica smiled.

"Tell me about it. Me, I've kinda given up on the idea that I'm gonna find some guy who's looking for a woman close to forty with two kids and no money. And if I did, I'd wonder what the hell was wrong with him."

"You never know," said Nica. "Maybe some guy will come along that's just dying for a family, will treat you and your

108

kids well and won't have three legs or an arm growing out of his neck."

"Look who's an optimist!" Colette laughed. "Nah, I figure it's me and them, and that's enough for me. It would be nice if a man fell from the sky, but I don't need some guy to rescue us. It's hard, but we're making it."

"You're a strong woman," said Nica.

"I just get up and go to work every day, and try to be there to make the kids breakfast in the morning and tuck them in at night."

"Half of the people in my business don't see their kids for days at a time," said Nica. "Sometimes weeks. That's half the reason I've never had any children of my own."

"That," said Colette, cleaning the last bit of biscuit from her plate, "and you hate men."

"I wish," Nica smiled. "Trouble is I love men, maybe too much. I want to trust them too easily, so instead I end up trusting none of them."

"So you really think I have another kid out there?" said Colette.

"Could be," said Nica. "Don't you want to know either way?"

"I dunno. What good can come of it? If I found out the kid died, it would break my heart. If he's alive, I'd feel like I had to find him. If he didn't want to see me, it would break my heart too. And if he did want to see me, I don't know what I would say."

"Am I keeping you from anything, Colette?"

She shook her head. "My day off, and the kids are spending the week at their grandma's ranch."

"Let's take a drive," said Nica.

* * *

They headed back into Denver, driving east away from the mountains and then south on the interstate. The afternoon traffic was thickening already.

"I lived in this crap hole of an apartment," said Colette, gazing out the window at the sleek, modern buildings, "over on the east side of town off Colfax. Not the nicest part of town back then, and it's only gotten worse."

"Is it still there, the place where you lived?"

"I think so, yeah."

"Can you remember how to get there?" asked Nica. Colette offered meandering directions that ultimately led them to a ramshackle extended stay motel that lay between a bath house and a convenience store.

"Wow," she said, craning her neck. "Guess the professionals have moved in. Looks like it's nothing but hookers and stuff now. Too bad. It was a dump even then, but I had some good memories."

"So this is where you lived when you first came to town?"

"Yeah," said Colette. "A couple of friends and I split a place. There was only one double bed, so two of us would share it at a time and the other one would sleep on the couch." She smiled wistfully. "I remember the hot water only lasted till about half-way through the second shower, so somebody always had to take one at night. And the only thing we had to cook with was this hot plate made out of cast iron or something. Could hardly heat up a cup of coffee on that damn thing."

"Sounds tough."

"I guess," Colette shrugged. "But we were on our own, all of us for the first time, so it didn't really matter. That's when I

110

saw the ad for the surrogate. It paid something like five thousand dollars, which was more money than any of us had ever seen. We all agreed we'd go get screened, and if one of us got picked, we'd split the money three ways."

"And so they picked you," said Nica.

"Yeah," she said, "lucky me. It's not too far if you wanna drive by where the agency used to be."

"Did they tell you who was looking for a surrogate?"

"I asked, but they wouldn't tell me anything. They just kept telling me I wouldn't be allowed to see the baby once it was born. Once, I overheard the physician in the hallway talking to some man I hadn't seen there before about an orphanage in town. Sounded like some religious name, saint something-or-other, but that didn't make any sense to me. I mean, why would someone pay a surrogate five thousand bucks to give birth to this kid, just to stick it in an orphanage?"

"That's a really good question," said Nica. "I think together we can try to figure that out." She pulled into a Kinko's a few blocks beyond an architecture firm and, after borrowing their phone book, made a copy of all of the churches listed in town. She tucked the small stack of papers in her file folder and looked over at Colette, who was gnawing at the fingernail of her index finger with her teeth.

"Tell you what," said Nica. "Why don't you come back with me to my hotel. We can make some calls to a few of these churches and see what we can find out. They have anything you could ever want from room service, and there's a Jacuzzi tub and everything. We can make it kind of a girls' night out."

"Sounds like more of a night in," Colette smiled.

"Let's make some calls first," said Nica, "then we'll go catch a movie, or go bowling, or do something stupid. My treat."

16

"Are you sure the scars are all gone?" asked Jacob, running his hands across Elena's wrists.

"Well, if you see something I don't," said Elena, "let me know."

"Maybe you used some kind of lotion or something," he said, opening Gus's medicine cabinet.

"Jacob, I've had these scars for, like, seven years. They wouldn't just disappear with a little bit of aloe."

"Well, then, what the hell happened?"

"I don't know," she said, "except that yesterday they were there and today they're gone."

"Yeah, I know," said Jacob. "You showed them to me. We were sitting out there on the couch."

They stared at one another in stunned silence.

"You don't think that I..." Jacob's words trailed off.

"All I know is you're the one who bleeds magically from his wrists, and you're the one who kissed me, right on my scars, and now, nothing."

"I didn't do anything," Jacob said.

"You're the one who has dreams about being Jesus for fuck's sake!"

"Yeah, and I also dream about flying sometimes! I'm not about to open the window and jump out to see if I really can!"

"I think it's time for us to go see Scratch," said Elena.

★ ★ ★

Scratch offered his hand to Elena. "Nice to see you again, my dear."

"You too, Scratch," said Elena. "Is it okay to call you that here?"

"Doesn't bother me," he said and smiled.

"Jacob really trusts you," said Elena, "and there have been some weird things going on lately. We're hoping you can help us understand what the hell is going on."

Scratch looked questioningly at Jacob.

"It's cool," said Jacob. "She knows about my dreams and everything."

"Has this to do with the gentleman who seems to be following you?" said Scratch.

"Gentleman's not the word I'd use for him," said Jacob.

"So is there some new development since I last heard?" asked Scratch.

"Yeah," said Jacob, "but not about the guy in the black suit." He nodded at Elena, who pushed up her sleeves. "See, she used to have these scars, right there," he pointed to her wrists. "I saw them there just yesterday, and today when she woke up, they were gone."

"Yes, I see nothing there," said Scratch. "So what's your question?"

"This wasn't like a scrape or something," said Elena. She glanced at Jacob, and then back at Scratch. "I had about a dozen stitches several years ago, along both wrists. I tried to kill myself."

"I'm sorry to hear that, though I'm glad that you feel comfortable enough to tell me."

"Well, you're a priest, right?" said Elena. "Don't people tell you this kind of stuff?"

"They do indeed."

"See, I hadn't exactly shown anyone my scars, figuring they'd think I was some kind of freak or something. But Jacob has been so sweet, I guess I felt comfortable with him."

"Especially considering my own baggage," Jacob rubbed at his forearms.

"He was so kind," Elena said, looking over at Jacob. "He just took my arms and kissed them. The next thing I knew, the scars were completely gone."

"I see," said Scratch. "So what do you think it is?"

"I don't know," Elena shrugged. "I'm not really a religious person, so I'm not even sure I know what a miracle is."

"The Catholic Church has many stipulations for what is and what isn't a miracle," said Scratch.

"But—" said Jacob. "I know you, and there's a 'but' coming." Scratch smiled.

"You've always been able to see my 'but' coming." Elena suppressed a giggle. "Yes," Scratch went on, "I'm not exactly one for all of the polity and dogma of the church."

"See," said Jacob, "that's why we get along. I don't even know what polity is, but the fact that you're not down with it even though your bosses say you're supposed to be is cool."

"In some cases," said Scratch, "the guidelines of the church serve a necessary purpose. In this case, however, I think if people think faithfully through it, they can discern what they think is miraculous for themselves in most cases."

"So what does all of that mean for us?" asked Elena.

"It means that it's up to you to decide if this was a miracle."

"But what is a miracle?" asked Elena.

"To me," said Scratch, "a miracle is anything that is beyond description, something that is wondrously outside the boundaries of human comprehension."

"But what about all this other stuff that's been going on with Jacob?" said Elena. "I mean, the dreams and all, and now this guy is following him everywhere? I don't understand what's going on."

"Unfortunately," said Scratch, "neither do I. But I want you to keep me posted. Tell me what is happening with this guy you think is following you and all the rest."

"Thanks Scratch," said Jacob, patting him on the shoulder. "Really."

"So where else are you kids off to today?"

"I gotta head to work," said Jacob. "I guess Elena's probably gonna hang out at Gus's place."

"Actually," said Elena, "If it's all right, I thought I might hang out at the store for a little bit."

"I'm sure Gus won't mind," said Jacob, "and it's not like you'll be getting in the way of all the customers." He leaned over and gave Scratch a hug. "Later, man."

"You kids stay out of trouble." Scratch smiled as they slipped out of his office.

After he heard the doors close behind them, Scratch eased himself into the chair behind his desk. His hand lingered over the telephone, reaching, and then pulling back.

Scratch placed his hand over his mouth, closed his eyes, took a breath, and picked it up.

"Hello. Yes, it's Father William. We have confirmation. It was a healing, just last night."

17

"So how long have you known the Essenoi exactly?" said Ya'aqov.

"Nearly twenty years now," Mariamne said. "I first came out here a couple of seasons after Yeshua's departure. He sent word for me, and throughout his time here, I came back occasionally to keep him apprised of how his family fared and other news."

"I know you explained why you didn't tell us," said Ya'aqov, wiping sweat from his forehead, leaving a reddish-brown smear across his brow, "but I can't help but have some resentment that you knew of his whereabouts and I didn't."

"As you certainly know," said Mariamne, "he always answered a higher call."

"Few, if any, realize the price paid by the loved ones of those who are called," he said.

"Gives you some empathy for what Maryam must have gone through."

"And poor father," said Ya'aqov, "has to reconcile the birth of a child that's not even his by blood, then raise him, have him leave inexplicably, and even deny him."

"You know he died loving all of you with his whole heart."

"Of course," Ya'aqov leaned against the side of the pit he was digging clay in, "but it doesn't mean it didn't pain him to do so."

"So how was your adventure up the cliffs with Benyamin?"

"I can hardly raise my arms above my head today," he groaned, "but it took getting all the way up there to understand why it is they go to the trouble."

"Sacred space," she said. "The Essenoi are believers in sacrifice. Not self-castigation, but sacrifice by looking beyond the wants of the physical world. For them, I think the journey up and down the cliffs is as sacred as the place itself."

"Seems so unnaturally out of the way."

"And faith isn't?" Mariamne laughed. "I mean, look at us!" She smeared a glob of clay on Ya'aqov's neck.

"I hate to interrupt," Benyamin said as he peered into the pit, "you two seem to be enjoying your chores."

"Sorry," said Ya'aqov. "We're falling back into old childhood habits, I suppose, and talking."

"Quite all right," said Benyamin. "Work does not have to be without joy. After all, if it is done in the name of the Lord, how can it be anything but joyful?"

"Clearly, you're more enlightened than I," said Ya'aqov, grinning.

"Come, Ya'aqov, shall we retreat to the caves to continue our studies together?"

"Maybe after a wash."

★ ★ ★

"I don't suppose," Ya'aqov said panting and out of breath as they stepped into the cave, "that you'd consider moving this Book of Remedies closer to the ground?"

"This cave has been its sacred resting place for more than two hundred years," said Benyamin. "Shall we relocate it because you are out of shape?" He let out a belly laugh that echoed across the valley.

"You're twice my age, and yet you have the energy to taunt me after the same climb," Ya'aqov said, collapsing against the cool rock of the cave wall.

"I'm only well-practiced." Benyamin settled into his seated position on the floor. "In time, you'll be at least as facile on these cliffs as I." He turned through the first pages of the codex, settling on a small body of text. "Here," he said, "this is a good place to begin."

"Anise and mint elixir?" Ya'aqov frowned. "This reads like a recipe. What am I supposed to learn from this?"

"This combination of herbs," said Benyamin, "taken as a concentrate or mixed into a tea, can help cure a number of ailments, from a cough to troubles with digestion."

"If I had a problem with either, I'd be grateful for the information. But as it is, I see no relevance to what I need to know as one who is carrying Yeshua's message to the rest of the world."

"What was one of Yeshua's greatest physical gifts to his faithful?" Benyamin asked.

"What," Ya'aqov grunted, "are you talking about healing?"

"Of course."

"But he didn't carry around a satchel full of anise, mint, and sandalwood," said Ya'aqov. "He simply laid his hands on people and they were healed. Sometimes they only reached out and touched a bit of his clothing, and in other cases, they weren't even there. Are you telling me this Book of Remedies was behind all of that?"

"Of course not," said Benyamin. "The Lord was behind that. However, Yeshua's journey of wisdom as a healer in many ways began right here."

"In a book full of herbal cures?" Ya'aqov snorted. "I think not."

"There is much more to this book than herbal remedies. Would you dare to appraise the state of all of Jerusalem simply by glancing at the front gates?"

"Fine," Ya'aqov sighed. "But I'll tell you now that I have no interest in learning the ways of healers."

"But you do seek to understand the ways of your brother. So you shall begin with this." Grumbling, Ya'aqov rested the codex in his lap, scanning over the first few pages. Benyamin closed his eyes and slipped into a meditative state, eyelids fluttering rapidly as his lips mouthed a silent prayer.

For hours, Ya'aqov read about the history of the great spiritual healers in the court of King Solomon, as well as the many elements from which they drew to offer health and well-being to the ruler's inner circle. As wisdom was passed from cleric to cleric, the degree of sophistication of their endeavors grew more complex.

By the time the sky shone in crimson and orange hues, Ya'aqov's mind was swimming with incantations to cure melancholy, meditations to provoke psychic and spiritual equilibrium, and even rituals to manipulate the elements, such as rainfall, fire, and control of systemic disease.

"I can't believe it," said Ya'aqov, closing the codex and rubbing his eyes. "Is all of this really true? Could they really do all of the things claimed in these pages?"

Benyamin opened his eyes, taking in a slow, deliberate breath.

"I was not there, of course," he said, unfolding his legs from their crossed position, "but I know that many of these are possible, as I have either seen them done or I have learned them myself."

"Your people can control the elements and cure people from demonic possession?"

"No," Benyamin smiled. "First of all, there are only a few so gifted that they have command over the volatile ways of the human mind and spirit. Even fewer ever have carried that power over to the world of inanimate elements. Much of this may have been theoretical, or it may truly have been achievable by some of Solomon's priests. At any rate, they had the benefit of a community who passed these secrets on from one generation to the next.

"Though we have possessed the Book of Remedies for some time now, it was bestowed upon us for safekeeping. We did not have the advantage of all of the communal wisdom that gave life to these words. We have learned what we could from it, but much of its power is beyond us. Only one among us ever has been fully enlightened by the book's wisdom."

"Yeshua," said Ya'aqov. Benyamin nodded. "Then why could he not teach you how to do what he did?"

"His mission was greater than becoming a mere teacher of the Essenoi."

"Since he never spoke of it," said Ya'aqov, "I thought the Lord simply endowed him with all of the gifts for ministry. It never occurred to me that he had to learn them."

18

"That was the most fun I've had since I can remember," said Colette on the way to Nica's car.

"It was fun," said Nica, "but I probably had one or two more drinks than I really needed!"

Nica drove until she spotted a drive-through coffee house, retrofitted from an old barn.

"Wow," said Nica, after ordering a pair of lattes, "it's hard to believe that this part of town was ever farming country, and even harder to imagine that a barn could have held up well enough to be made into this."

"What, this?" Colette peered out her window at the young, clean-cut employees scurrying around. "Nah, this used to be the old beer barn. It was kind of the gateway to the east side. I would walk over here sometimes to hang out."

"Drive-through beer barn?"

"Welcome to the wild west," Colette smiled. "We do things a little different here."

"It's funny." Nica handed the cups across to Colette, who sniffed them suspiciously. "Growing up in New York, you think you see a little bit of everything. But it's in its own little bubble, just like everywhere else. You think you know what the world is like, and then you step outside of your comfort zone and suddenly you're in some parallel universe."

"Yeah, okay," Colette raised an eyebrow, "whatever you say. I guess I don't really think a beer barn is that weird."

Nica turned right just past an elementary school, noticing what appeared to be the church ahead. "There we go," she said, pulling into an open parking spot on the opposite side of the street. Colette sighed anxiously. "You all right?" Nica said.

"I guess," Colette said. "I just...I don't know. What if we find this kid and he doesn't want to even talk to me? Or what if he's dead, or maybe it's a she and she's dead?"

"Hey," Nica said, putting a comforting hand on her shoulder, "I think what you're going through is perfectly normal. It's a lot to take in."

Colette began to cry.

"Why don't we hang out here," said Nica. "At least until we finish our—wait a second—" Colette looked up at Nica, who was watching a young man and woman come out of the front doors of the church.

"I know this is going to sound completely crazy," said Nica, "but I think that young man over there might be your son." Colette craned her neck around Nica.

"Seriously?" she said. "He doesn't look very much like me. Why would you say that? I mean, they could be anybody."

"I don't exactly have time to explain," said Nica, "but based on what I know about the fertility study done with you, I'm almost positive your child was a boy, and his paternal genetic line would have been from the Middle East."

"You mean his dad was an Arab?"

"I guess you could say that," Nica whipped the car around in the middle of the street and pulled up within a dozen feet of the young couple, walking along the sidewalk. "Just go with whatever I do, okay?" Colette nodded her consent, her eyes fixed on the couple.

"Excuse me," Nica said as she rolled down her window. "Do you know how to get to the convention center?"

Elena and Jacob looked at each other and smiled.

"Yeah, you're pretty much on the wrong side of town for that," said Jacob.

"I know, I got off the highway and tried to remember the directions this guy gave me, but I must have done something wrong. You guys heading downtown?"

"Yeah," said Jacob, "we're catching the bus."

"Hop in if you want," said Nica. "I'll save you the bus fare if you can help me figure out where I'm going."

Jacob checked his watch and looked at Elena.

"I'm running kinda late for work," he said, "so yeah, a ride would be nice."

Jacob opened the back door to the car and they climbed in.

"I'm Nica, and this is my friend, Colette."

"Jacob. This is Elena."

They shook hands.

"Thanks for the ride," said Elena.

"Hey, I'd rather have you guys show me the way than have to stop every three blocks to ask directions again. You guys from around here?"

"Yeah, I am," said Jacob. "I actually grew up right back there," he pointed back toward the church.

"You grew up in a church?" Nica said.

"There's an orphanage connected to it. I just go back sometimes to visit, you know. We both live in town now."

"I'm actually from Loveland," said Elena, "a little farther north."

"I'm from Manhattan," said Nica.

"No kidding?" Elena's eyes got big. "I always wanted to go there. It looks awesome."

"It is pretty great," said Nica.

"Turn left up here in two more blocks," said Jacob, "and then left on the next street."

"So you grew up in a church home," said Nica. "That must have been interesting. I went to Catholic school for a while myself."

"Yeah, it was different, I guess," he said. "I mean, I don't really know, since I never went anywhere else, but hearing people talk about public school and stuff, it's definitely different being taught by nuns."

"I still have scars on my knuckles," said Nica. They drove in silence for a few moments. "I'm actually in town working on a story about young people in Denver and how life for them is different than in the Big Apple."

"You're a writer?"

Nica nodded. "Reporter. For the New Yorker magazine."

Jacob and Elena glanced at each other.

"I'd love to talk to you guys some more about your experiences here. Are you free for dinner, by any chance? My treat, of course."

"I have to work until about six," said Jacob, "but I guess we could do something after that." Nica handed them each a business card.

"Here's how you can reach me," she said. "My cell number's at the bottom there. Just give me a ring when you're off and we'll meet up wherever you want."

"Cool," said Jacob, sliding the card into his pocket.

"Do you have a number where I can find you?" said Nica.

"Just in case something comes up, or I get lost on the other side of town again."

"Got a pen?" Jacob scribbled down a set of numbers on the back of an old bus ticket. "This is for Modulation Records, right up there, where I work," he pointed half a block up on the right toward the brick structure. "We're crashing at a friend's place for a while, or else I'd give you my home number."

"Oh," said Nica, "okay. Not staying at the co-op?"

"It's kind of a long story," said Jacob. "Maybe at dinner."

Nica pulled over in front of the store.

"It was a great coincidence, running into you two," she said.

"Sure," said Jacob. "Thanks for the ride. You just have to keep going along this street for a few blocks, turn right on Speer, and you can't miss the convention center."

★ ★ ★

"They seemed nice," said Elena.

"Yeah," Jacob said. "That one lady didn't say much. Just kept staring at me, like she was stoned or something."

"Maybe she's just shy."

"A shy reporter?"

"I dunno," Jacob sighed. "That Nica chick seemed cool, but there was something weird about what's-her-name."

"Colette?"

"Yeah, Colette. Just got a weird vibe."

Gus glanced at his watch as Jacob and Elena came through the front door. "Mark this day down," he said, eyebrows raised. "Jacob Venable is early to work. You looking for a raise or something?"

"We grabbed a ride from some lady," Jacob said. "Otherwise

I would have probably been late."

"That's more like it," said Gus. "You can't go messing with my worldview like that."

"Hey, is it cool if Elena hangs here for a while?"

"Actually," Elena said, "I might go back to Gus's place and crash for a while, if that's cool." Gus shrugged.

★ ★ ★

"Do you really think that was my son?" Colette stared bleary-eyed at Nica.

"I have to make sure," said Nica, "but I have a good feeling."

"How do you make sure?"

"DNA test," said Nica. "I have to get him to swab his mouth and let me send the sample off to my associate in Germany."

Colette rested her head against the seat.

"This is all so mysterious and strange. What's going on, really, and how is it that you think you know who my son is?"

"That will take some explaining," Nica sighed. "Let's head back to the hotel for a while." Nica's phone rang just as they reached the room at the Ambassador. She reached for it.

"You causing plenty of trouble?" Edward said.

"That's what they pay me for, isn't it?"

"Well, you must have crapped in somebody's nest," he said. "I got a call from some anonymous guy this morning, telling me I'd better pull you off this story before something unfortunate happens to you."

"Unfortunate," she repeated. "Like I might slip on a banana peel?"

"I told him to come down here himself and I'd show him unfortunate."

"Thanks, Eddie," Nica said. "You're a sweetheart."

"You sure everything's cool down there?"

"So far," she said. "I'm here with Colette. She's been helping me out."

"Colette," Edward said. "Sounds hot."

"I wouldn't say that's exactly accurate," said Nica. "She's the mom I told you about."

"What about the kid?"

"Dinner tonight," said Nica. "I still have a lot of explaining to do to get everybody on the same page."

* * *

Back at the hotel room, Colette watched Nica anxiously.

"Want anything from room service?" Nica asked.

"No, I'm fine," said Colette.

"Need to make any calls?"

"No, really, I'm good. I just want to know what you know about my kid."

"Right," said Nica. "You might want to sit down for this."

Nica proceeded to explain everything she knew about The Project, their interest in the fulfillment of scripture through the controversial genetics experiment, as well as her role in it. As she spoke, Colette's eyes got wider. After almost fifteen minutes of straight talking, Nica paused. Colette sagged in her chair as if she were a ball that had been punctured.

"I can't believe this," Colette whispered. "Why would they pick me, hoping he'd be the second coming of Jesus Christ?"

"They wanted someone near an orphanage connected to a church," said Nica, "and I get the feeling they wanted a less obvious choice of locations, too. Denver's big enough to be anonymous in, but pretty out of the way as far as cities go."

"But why did they even risk letting him live out in the real world, then?" said Colette. "Why didn't they just raise him in a lab somewhere, or...?"

"They didn't know if the experiment would actually work," said Nica. "I think that they wanted to let him grow up in as much of a normal environment as possible, while not giving up too much control over his upbringing. They wanted to kind of observe the signs they were looking for, too."

"Signs? What kind of signs?"

"I don't know," Nica gazed at the fan blades spinning above her. "That's part of what I hope to find out at dinner tonight. If anything strange has been going on, hopefully I can get him to share that."

19

After a quiet meal together, the Essenoi surrounded Mariamne, laid their hands upon her, and offered a blessing. She gave Ya'aqov a long embrace, followed by a tearful goodbye, and then she was on her way.

Navigating her way up toward the crest of the mountain range, Mariamne thought about Ya'aqov panting behind Benyamin as they climbed the cliffs. Her mind drifted back through the years to the first time she met Yeshua there. She was as frail and slender as he was bony and clumsy, yet they shared a bond as if they were woven in the same womb. Every time she left him there, she wept, and he would place a hand on her forehead, lessening the pain of separation somewhat. She would burn with eagerness to tell someone of his whereabouts, but would bite her tongue, yearning for the next time he summoned her.

Mariamne recalled the elation she felt when he finally returned for good, eighteen years later, a man ready to set aside all earthly longings, including her love, for a greater call to which he was drawn. For three years, she listened intently to his teaching, all the while nurturing an emptiness within herself that she knew never would be filled. Mariamne ached at the thought of his death, pinned to a cross like a criminal, drained of his vitality only after being stripped of human dignity.

By the time the sun reached its height, Mariamne had completed more than half of the journey home. She came over the crest of a rocky hill and looked down upon the great city. Ribbons of smoke wove swirling patterns above the houses, combining into a thin, brown haze. Mariamne steadied herself as she stepped from one rock to another along the downward slope, too mindful of her own footsteps to notice the figures approaching as she reached the flat below.

"You," said a stern voice from atop a towering horse. "Woman, you there!" The legionnaire and another Roman soldier rode astride one another, pulling up just in front of her. "Where have you come from?"

"I am from Magdala," Mariamne said, "but my home is in Jerusalem."

"That's not the question, woman," said the smaller soldier. "Where have been?"

"We're looking for a man," the legionnaire said. "Perhaps you know him? His name is Ya'aqov, son of Yosef and Maryam."

Mariamne glanced up, and then quickly cast her eyes back toward her feet.

"Ya'aqov is a dear friend," Mariamne said, "a brother…"

"He's a traitor to the Roman government is what he is," the legionnaire said. "Unless you want to suffer the same fate that awaits him and the rest of the Christian traitors, you'll tell us where he is."

Mariamne closed her eyes and said nothing.

"What's wrong?" sneered the soldier. "Aren't you the one they call Mariamne? Word around here is that you're fearless."

The smaller soldier dismounted and came around behind

her, shoving her toward his horse with his armor-clad forearm.

"Get on," he growled next to her ear, "before I have to do anything you'd regret."

★ ★ ★

The warden of the cluster of holding cells was a grizzled, filthy man with half of his teeth rotted from neglect. When he spoke, his voice gurgled with phlegm.

"What do we have today, gents?" he said, smiling crookedly at the legionnaires.

"An enemy of Rome," said the soldier. "She knows the location of Ya'aqov, brother of Yeshua. It's up to you to find out where he is before we return tomorrow."

His partner shoved Mariamne with his shoulder, leaning toward the back of his horse, causing her to tumble to the dirt, face-down.

"Don't kill her if you can help it," the legionnaire man said. "I'd like to have a go at whatever's left if she lives through the night."

Mariamne kept her face close to the ground, masking her tears.

"I've got special accommodations for you, dear," he hissed, dragging her toward a vacant cell. The small chamber was barely long enough in each direction for her to lie down, and the floor was covered with a thin, matted layer of straw that reeked of human waste. Mariamne wretched from the smell, collapsing to her knees from the involuntary spasms that accompanied her illness.

"Now, that's no way to show gratitude," said the warden, wiping his chin with his sleeve. "Especially after I went and gave you the nicest one of the lot." He slammed the iron gate shut, resting his forearms on the crossbar. "I'll be back for you in a bit. It's going to be a long night, my lovely."

Once the warden was out of sight, Mariamne burst into sobs, pulling at her hair as she wailed. "Yeshua!" she called out. "Yeshua, give me strength!" As her crying subsided, she rested her forehead against her hands and began to rock back and forth as she prayed. The warden's hacking finally drew her out of her meditative state.

"What's the matter with you?" he said, saliva spraying out from the gaps in his mouth. "You look like you've seen a ghost." He snorted mockingly as he unlocked the gate. "Now, are you going to come along peacefully, or are you going to require some convincing?" Mariamne slowly pulled herself to her feet, keeping her eyes fixed on her feet as she walked. "That's a girl," he sneered. "You cooperate like this, and we'll be thick as thieves by morning."

He led her to a room with only two chairs, a table, and a glowing cast iron stove. On the table was an assortment of carpentry and blacksmith tools, including an awl, a wooden mallet, an iron hammer, several pairs of tongs, and three leather straps. The warden sat her in the chair, binding her ankles with one strap and her wrists with another. The smell of his unwashed body made her eyes water. When the warden noticed the tears, he turned his mouth into a mocking frown.

"Deary," he said, stroking her hair, "no need to waste all of those tears so soon. We've not even begun. There will be plenty of reason to cry in time, but we're just getting to know each other. Let's start with where you're from."

He straddled her calves, lifting her ankles from the ground with one arm and pressing a hot coal grasped in a pair of tongs against the bottom of her feet with the other. Mariamne let out a scream so shrill that the warden dropped the tongs.

"Love," Mariamne whispered.

"What's that?" said the warden.

"Love," she said again, louder this time.

"It's come to my attention that you're close with the family of Yeshua. I know where everyone you hold dear in Jerusalem is sleeping tonight. And right outside those doors," he pointed back to where they had come into the room, "is a messenger that's waiting for a word from me and he'll be off."

"Qumran," Mariamne whispered. The warden grinned as he let her hair go.

"Now, see," he said, stepping back away from her. "One simple word, and you saved a dozen lives or more. That's more than your Christ ever did. Aren't you proud to have such miraculous power?"

The warden walked around behind Mariamne and picked up a hammer. A moment later it landed on the base of her skull with a bone-splitting crack.

20

Sid's Italian Café was a dimly lit space with high ceilings, high-backed burgundy benches, and small tables with old wine labels varnished onto the surface. Along the walls were photographs of Sid, the owner, with celebrities who had dined there over the years, including Dean Martin and Don Rickles. Music from the Rat Pack played in the background, and each table was adorned with a single white rose. Though it was out of his price range, Jacob enjoyed the infrequent opportunity to absorb the mafia-esque atmosphere. When he came through the door, Nica and Colette were waiting for him in a corner booth. He looked around for Elena, and finding no sign of her, headed for the booth.

"Nice choice of restaurants," Nica said.

"I hope it's not too pricey," said Jacob.

"No, this is fine," Nica said. "I'm on an expense account, and compared to New York, Denver prices are very affordable. Is your girlfriend coming?"

"Yeah, she should be here soon," he said. "She crashed back at Gus's place for a while. All of the drama the last few days kinda wore her out, I think."

"Drama?" said Nica. "What kind of drama?"

"Well," he said, "my room at the co-op got busted into the

other day, and since then, we've been pretty much out of sorts."

"Do you know who did it?"

"Actually, yeah," he said. "We got the guy's name and where he's staying."

"No kidding?"

"Yeah, my friend Allen lifted a receipt from his pocket, which led us to his room at the Ambassador Hotel."

"That's where I'm staying," said Nica.

"No shit?" he said. "Sorry, I mean, that's interesting. That's totally weird that you're in the same place as this guy. It's like we're all connected or something."

"Maybe so," said Nica.

The waiter took their drink orders, and then Nica turned back to Jacob, who was glancing at Colette, her face still buried in the menu.

"So Jacob, tell me about how you ended up at the co-op."

"I wish I knew more," he said, "but my background is a little sketchy."

Colette peered out from behind her menu.

"I grew up at Sacred Heart orphanage, which is a part of the church where we met earlier. When I turned eighteen, they gave me a little bit of money to get out on my own, and pretty much all I could afford was the co-op. Since then, I've been working at Modulation Records, playing gigs when I can, and trying to figure out what to do with my life."

"Gigs?" Nica said. "You're a musician?"

"Yeah, I play saxophone. Jazz mostly."

"How did you get into jazz?" asked Nica. "Seems like an unlikely choice of styles for a young kid."

Jacob told the story about Scratch and the gift of the horn. He talked about the hours he spent in Scratch's office listening to Dizzy Gillespie and John Coltrane. As he spoke, he seemed transported, his features softening and his eyes drifting around the room, as if he were retracing his life story through invisible music notation.

"If Scratch hadn't given me that horn and played all those records for me," said Jacob, "I don't know what I'd be doing."

"Sounds like a special guy," said Nica. Jacob nodded, glancing at Colette.

"So, is she, like, your assistant or something?"

"Colette is a good friend," said Nica, placing a hand on her forearm. "She's helping me find my way around town, and she had some interest in hearing more about your story."

"Okay," he said. "Whatever."

"Do you know much about your parents?" asked Nica.

Jacob shook his head. "I asked a few times when I was younger, but all they would tell me was that my file was sealed."

"Did you ever live with foster families or have any families consider adoption?"

"You know," Jacob gave a half-smile, "I used to kinda have a complex because it seemed like all these kids came and went, but nobody wanted me. But after a while, I just chalked it up to my age. Everybody wants babies. They don't really want to take on an older kid."

"Do you ever wonder who your parents are?" said Colette.

"I guess," he said. "Sure. I mean, anybody would be curious, but I just didn't figure there was much sense in putting too much energy into something that would never change. There's really no way for me to know, so why worry about it?"

"I have a confession," said Nica. "It wasn't entirely by accident that we ran into each other today."

"What do you mean?"

"Well, I was coming to that church to try to find some more information about you, actually."

"Me?" Jacob leaned back. "But you don't even know me."

"Maybe," said Nica, "but this story I've been working on has led me to you. If I told you I might be able to help you learn more about where you came from, would you be interested?"

Jacob sat silently. He looked back toward the door again, furrowing his eyebrows.

"She should have been here by now," he said. "Maybe she's still sleeping."

"Elena?" asked Nica, reaching for her phone. "Do you want to give her a call?"

"I would, but I don't have Gus's home number."

"Maybe she's just getting ready," she smiled. "You know how we girls can be."

"Yeah, maybe."

"I know this is a little confusing, but there are ways to try to figure out who you really are, that is, if you want to know."

"Well, yeah," he said. "I guess so. I hadn't really thought about it, but who wouldn't want to know where they came from?"

"I have a friend," she said, "a scientist. If I send him a sample, he can do a genetic analysis and help determine a whole lot about who you are."

"Sample," he said. "Like pee in a cup or something?"

"Actually, all you have to do is run this little swab along the inside of your cheek." She pulled a baggie containing two Q-Tips out of her purse. "I'll express mail it to him, and by tomorrow evening he'll tell me whatever he finds out."

"Is this some sort of scam or something," he said, "because I don't have any money."

"No, I'll take care of all of the costs."

"And why would you do that?"

"You'll have to trust me a little bit," she said, "but I have my own reasons for wanting to know where you came from." She set the baggie on the table.

Jacob took out one of the swabs, stroked it along the inside of his cheek, put it back in the baggie and handed it to her.

"There," he said. "Free crap from my mouth in exchange for you coming clean about what you really want."

They placed their orders and Nica began to explain the steps that had led her to him. Jacob listened intently, his expression unchanging as she spoke. He ignored his food when it came, fixed on her story about The Project, the titulus crucis, somatic cell nuclear transfers, the fertility clinic, and the surrogate.

"So now are you gonna tell me I've been sitting here having dinner with my mom?"

"Well, yes," said Nica. "I guess that is what I'm saying. Jacob, meet Colette, your mother."

Jacob scowled. "You guys are full of shit," he said. "I don't know what your angle is, but this is too bizarre to be for real."

"I know it's a lot to take in," Nica said, "but let me ask you about this man who has been following you."

"Haman," said Jacob, "the guy in the black suit."

"Right, Haman. Has he actually stolen anything from you?"

"No, I guess not." Jacob paused. "I mean, he sort of tore up the sheets from my bed when he trashed my room, but that's all."

"Has he tried to hurt you at all?"

"Well, no, unless you count when he chased us after we broke into his room at the hotel."

"Why do you think he might have been interested in your

sheets?"

"I dunno," Jacob shrugged. "I mean there was some..." he looked down at his plate.

"What is it?"

"There was blood on them, all right?"

"Blood?"

"Yeah, blood," he said, pulling his sleeves up to reveal the wounds on his wrists. Nica gasped and Colette's hands trembled as she brought her hands to her face.

"Dear God," said Colette.

"It's not that big of a deal, really," said Jacob. "It happens sometimes."

"So this has happened before?" said Nica. "Involuntarily?"

"If you're asking if I've tried to kill myself," he looked at her impatiently, "the answer is no. Usually, it happens when I'm asleep."

"Is there anything else unusual that accompanies this?" Nica asked.

"I have these dreams," he said. "I'm, like, back in Jesus' time or something. Sometimes they're different, but usually they have something to do with crucifixion."

"Anything else?"

"Well, there is this thing with Elena," he said looking nervously toward the door. "She really should be here by now."

"Jacob," said Nica, "what thing with Elena are you talking about?"

Jacob shook his head. "It's probably nothing," he said, "but she had these scars on her arms, and one night I sort of kissed them," his cheeks reddened. "And then the next day, when she woke up, they were gone."

"Do you find all of this a little unusual?"

"Well, that's a stupid fucking question," he snapped. "Of course I find it unusual. But what the hell am I supposed to do about it?"

"That's why I'm here," said Nica. "I want to help you figure out where you came from, and if I can, I want to help you do something about it."

"You're here to write a story," he said. "I appreciate your effort to act generous and everything, but if I didn't have something you wanted, you wouldn't be here."

"But by the same token, if all of this wasn't going on, you wouldn't be in possible danger either."

"Right," he said, "so you're my own personal savior, huh?"

"I'm no saint," said Nica, "but I do want to help you." Her phone rang in her purse and she reached for it. "Isn't three-zero-three a Denver area code?" she asked. Colette nodded. Nica held the phone to her ear.

"Yes, this is she," she said, followed by a pause. "Who is speaking?" she looked up at Jacob. "Yes, he is, but if you don't..." she paused again. "Fine." She handed the phone to Jacob. "It's for you."

Jacob held the phone to his ear, his expression hardening while he listened. His eyes smoldered with rage as he sat quietly. He leaned his head against his hand, closing his eyes before flipping the phone closed. He slid the phone across the table and sat for a moment in stunned silence.

"What is it?" said Nica. "Was that him? Was that Haman?"

Jacob nodded. "I have to go," he said, standing up out of the booth. "I have to go back and see Scratch."

"Why? What did he say?"

"Haman has Elena," Jacob said. "If I don't meet him tomorrow night at Sacred Heart Church, he's going to kill her."

"My God," said Colette.

"We'll go with you," said Nica. "We can use my car."

* * *

"You've got me a little worried," said Scratch. "What's going on?"

"Scratch," said Jacob, "this is Nica. She's a reporter for the New Yorker magazine. And this is Colette. She's, well, my mom. Maybe. I think."

"Your mother?" Scratch looked at Colette, then at Jacob and back to Colette.

"Yeah," Jacob sighed, "it's a little complicated."

"And the New Yorker?"

"They want to do this story about me, possibly," Jacob said, "and all this weird stuff that's been going on."

"I'm afraid I don't understand," Scratch rubbed his chin anxiously as he leaned back in his chair.

"Well, here's the long and short of it. The guy in black, he's the bad guy. He's trying to get something from me or do something to me—I don't know, but it's bad, okay? So I was at dinner with them, talking about all of this stuff and, out of the blue, he calls Nica's phone."

"Who?"

"The bad guy, Scratch," Jacob said impatiently. "The man in black. Damn, keep up man."

"Sorry."

"So somehow he got her number, probably from somebody at her office, and he calls and asks for me. Then he basically threatens me if I don't do what he says."

"What kind of threat?"

"He kidnapped Elena. He's going to kill her, and if I don't follow his directions, he'll kill me, too."

"My goodness," whispered Scratch. "What has he asked you to do?"

"He wants me to meet him here tomorrow night at ten o'clock."

"Here?"

"That's what he said."

"Do you have any idea why he would ask to meet at this church?" said Nica.

"I don't know," said Scratch. "If he's looking for information about Jacob, maybe he hopes to leverage Elena to get at his files. But after a child graduates from the program or gets adopted, their paperwork is forwarded to the local bishop's office."

"What about you?" Nica said.

"What about me?" asked Scratch.

"Has this guy tried making contact with you at all?"

Scratch shook his head. "I've never heard of this Haman guy in my life before Jacob told me about him. I think we should call the police."

"He said if we do, he'll kill her before he even comes inside the building," said Jacob.

"He told Jacob that if he sees anyone but you and him," Nica said, "Elena's dead."

"The last thing I want to do is put anyone's life at risk," said Scratch, "Let's see what he has to say. Maybe we can reason with him. After all, you're no good to him dead."

"That's why I came to you," said Jacob. "I figure you'd know what to do."

"Come back tomorrow night, alone," said Scratch, "and in

the meantime, call me if you learn anything else, or if you need me for absolutely anything." Scratch and Jacob embraced, and Nica shook his hand as they departed.

"Thanks for your help, Father," said Nica.

21

"This is so messed up," moaned Jacob from the front seat of Nica's car. "This is all my fault."

"How is any of this your fault, Jacob?" Nica said. "You can't help how you were conceived, or where you were raised."

"Elena's the victim, not me," he said and leaned back against the headrest. "If I hadn't dragged her into all of this, she'd be fine right now."

"You can't blame yourself," said Nica. "All you can try to do now is get her back safely."

"If anything happens to her, I swear I'll kill that son of a bitch myself."

"I have a question for you," Nica said, "and I want you to try to really think about this, rather than just getting mad, okay?"

"That's kind of a setup, isn't it?"

"I'm just curious," she said, "but have you ever actually told Scratch Haman's name?"

"Yeah, I told him about how he broke into my room, and how we tracked him down and everything."

"But did you ever actually tell him the man's name?"

"I don't think so, why?"

"I noticed back at the church that you only described him as 'the bad guy,' or 'the guy in black,' and then when he referred to Haman, he used his name."

"Yeah, so?"

"So if you didn't ever tell him his name, how did he know it?"

"I don't know," Jacob sighed. "Maybe he's psychic. Maybe God told him."

"There's one other thing," said Nica. "Just before we left, he said something about you not being any good to him dead."

"Yeah, I remember."

"But you didn't explain to him everything that I told you tonight about The Project and the situation surrounding your birth. He has no way of knowing whether this Haman guy wants you alive or dead, unless…"

"Wait," Jacob held up his hand, "don't tell me you're thinking that Scratch has something to do with all of this?"

"Well, you tell me," said Nica. "Aside from those two things, how do you think Haman found Elena? Who else have you told where you're staying?"

"Just Allen, a friend at the co-op."

"Okay, so Allen could have told him," said Nica, "but didn't you tell me that Allen was the one who stole the receipt that led you to Haman in the first place?"

"Yeah, he did."

"And if you think about it, it makes perfect sense that Scratch might be involved. After all, he helped raise you, and he's connected to the orphanage where you were placed after you were born. He's known you your whole life, right?"

"Yeah," said Jacob, "but he's like my dad, or at least the closest I have. I mean, Scratch loves me."

"I hope so," said Nica, "and I'd love to find out I'm wrong. But I have a bad feeling about him."

"Even if he is involved," said Jacob, "what fucking difference

145

does it make now? All I want is to get Elena back and to get the hell away from this guy."

Nica picked up her phone and scrolled through her address book when she came to a stop light. "I don't think it's safe for you to stay at Gus's place tonight," she said. "Why don't you come with us to the hotel?"

"Right," Jacob laughed bitterly, "let's go hang out at the hotel where Haman is staying. I don't think so. Remember, I got run out of that place. They're probably still looking for me."

"What about my house," said Colette. "It should be safe there." Nica nodded.

"Whatever, man," he said, closing his eyes. "Mom knows best."

"We didn't really end up eating at Sid's," Nica said, glancing at her phone. "Should we pick something up on the way to Colette's place?"

"I'm not hungry," said Jacob, "but go ahead and call for pizza or whatever if you want."

"Actually," she said, "that conversation at the church gave me an idea, but I have to call a friend back in New York first."

She flipped through her list of names and dialed Frederick. "Freddie," Nica said when he picked up, "this is Nica. How's the Grindhouse treating you? Great. Listen, I don't think I'm going to be able to make your party this weekend, but I need a little bit of advice, and I think you have just the kind of expertise I need."

22

"**M**ariamne!" Ya'aqov called out, blinded by the darkness that surrounded him. He sat up from his palette on the ground, grasping at the air until his head began to clear.

"Is there something wrong?" said Benyamin, his voice coming from the other side of the half-wall that separated them. "Are you all right, Ya'aqov?"

"I—yes, I'm fine," he said, still panting for air. "I apologize for waking you. I was having a terrible dream."

"Oh?"

"Something happened to Mariamne!"

Ya'aqov laid his head back down, the stars above him gradually coming into focus.

"We sent her home with our prayers," said Benyamin. "That is all we can do. For now, you should try to get some more rest."

Ya'aqov sighed and tried to calm his leaping heart as traces of the dream lingered in his consciousness.

"I'm sure it was nothing," he said, closing his eyes, waiting for sleep to return.

★ ★ ★

In the morning, the cool air combined with Ya'aqov's restlessness from the dream, causing him to oversleep. By the time he stirred, he was alone in the commune, each of the Essenoi already about their daily chores. Grabbing a pomegranate from a basket in the dining area, Ya'aqov wandered down to the water. He saw Mariamne's face in every surface.

"Yeshua," he said aloud as he sucked the pulp off a pomegranate seed, "if it is the Lord's will, I ask that you keep our dear friend safe. It is not for my sake, but for the cause that I ask this. She is a strong, faithful woman, and this world, rife with madmen as it is, is all the better with her in it."

The cry of sea birds careened off the rocks around him as Ya'aqov spotted a cluster of gulls bursting from a nearby cove.

"Did you see that?" said Benyamin from behind Ya'aqov.

"Saints and sinners, Ben! Why do you sneak up on me like that?"

Benyamin laughed, slapping Ya'aqov on the back. He pointed toward the point on horizon from where the birds had come.

"Did you see them?"

"Of course," said Ya'aqov, "what of them? Are they some special sort of bird or something?"

Ben shook his head.

"They are frightened," he said, squinting into the sun. "They feel something we cannot yet detect."

"Frightened? Of what?"

"Not sure," said Ben. "Could be a storm coming. Could be predators. Who knows? But something is coming."

"Well that's helpful," said Ya'aqov. "Let's prepare ourselves for 'something.'" He squinted at the horizon. "So what's on our schedule today?"

"I thought we'd walk," Ben strode along the water's edge, gesturing for Ya'aqov to follow.

"Fine," said Ya'aqov. "Where to?"

"Don't know yet. I suppose we'll find out when we get there."

"And how will you know we've gotten there?" Ya'aqov asked.

"Because we'll stop," he said, quickening his pace.

"Of all the wise men I could have learned from in this great world," said Ya'aqov, "I had to end up with a village idiot who wants to walk everyone to death!"

Benyamin led Ya'aqov along the boundary of the water until he veered left. They climbed along a ridge of rocks that snaked between two fields of jagged boulders. At first, the climb was easy and the slope gradual, but as they progressed, the footholds became more perilous and the incline caused Ya'aqov's legs and arms to burn.

"Why, if you don't even have a destination in mind," huffed Ya'aqov, "would you choose such an unforgiving path?"

"To see with new eyes," said Ben, bounding from the top of one craggy stone to another. "If we went the easy way, we'd only see what plenty of others had already seen before us."

"Great," said Ya'aqov, "but is it worth seeing with new eyes if I lose a limb in the process?"

Ben did not slow his ascent.

After more than an hour, they neared the summit of a barren, flat mountain that overlooked the valley on the other side of the range from where the Essenoi resided. Benyamin scanned the view intently.

"Look," said Benyamin, angling his hand toward a spot in the far distance. "The birds were right."

"What?" said Ya'aqov. "I don't see a thing." Ben motioned for Ya'aqov to stand alongside him, orienting his eyes to a shadowy cluster that was moving slightly along the farthest visible rim of the desert.

"They were right," he said again. "Something is coming, or rather, someone."

"It appears to be men on horseback," said Ya'aqov. "Most likely Roman sentries."

"Oh? Why do you say that?"

"Because they're the only ones stupid enough to ride their horses across the desert," snorted Ya'aqov. He looked heavenward, squinting into the glare. "They're coming for me," he said.

"I suppose we'll find out when they get here," said Ben.

"No," Ya'aqov looked at Ben. "I can't be responsible for bringing them here. You're not even armed. If they have an inclination to, they could wipe out the whole lot of you."

"If it's our time," said Ben, "we will accept what will come to us."

"Well you may be all right with dying," Ya'aqov began to ease himself back down the rocks, "but I'm not going to be responsible for that happening today."

"What would you do, then?"

"We'll go back to camp," Ya'aqov offered a hand to Ben. "I have a few things to leave in your care. Then I'll head back in their direction and hopefully meet them before they catch sight of your camp."

"Surely the sight of our home isn't enough cause to invoke a slaughter?"

"If they consider me to be a criminal," said Ya'aqov, "which they do, then you're harboring an enemy of the state."

"You do not need to concern yourself with our welfare," Benyamin followed him down the slope. "We have taken care of ourselves for a very long time."

"This is more about what I feel the need to do than it is about your principles of peace," said Ya'aqov. "Though I respect your willingness to open your home to me regardless of the cost, I cannot in good conscience allow such a massacre to take place on my account. Either way, they'll get what they came for. It's best for me to go."

"I will not argue with you," said Ben, "but we will never ask you to leave, regardless of the consequence."

"Maybe you did teach Yeshua a thing or two about faithfulness," smiled Ya'aqov as he stumbled toward the seaside.

* * *

Back in the camp, Ya'aqov found his leather satchel and, handing it to Benyamin, his eyes welled with sorrow. "This is all that is left," he said.

"Of what?"

"Yeshua. This is all he left behind."

"Hardly." Benyamin placed his arm around Ya'aqov. "What your brother left behind in this world will forever change it. These physical reminders may be modest, but the effect of his ministry is already set into motion. It is indelible."

"I hope and pray," Ya'aqov sighed, "for all our sakes, that you're right."

He opened the top of the bag and pulled out the bowl, the tools, and the titulus crucis.

"I don't know if you want to hold onto this or not," said Ya'aqov. "It's a bit morbid, and I intended to get rid of it many times, as all it reminds me of is the suffering he endured at the end. However, I've never brought myself to actually do it."

"If you leave it in our care," Ben said, "it will be kept safe and preserved well. We will return it to its rightful owner on that glad day when you return to us."

* * *

By the time he reached the top of the surrounding ridge, Ya'aqov could see the bronze breastplates of the legionnaires glinting in the desert sunlight, the trail behind the passel of horses consumed by a billowing cloud of dust. The man in front, a centurion, bore the red horsehair brush that signaled his position of leadership within the group.

As Ya'aqov reached the base of the mountain on the other side, two men on horseback rode up hastily to meet him. Their faces, red like the pomegranate seeds he had for breakfast, were drenched in sweat and contorted with fatigue.

"You lads oughtn't wear so many unnecessary vestments for this kind of travel," Ya'aqov said, "unless the object of your search is someone more threatening than I."

"Ya'aqov bar Yosef," said one of the legionnaires, "son of Maryam, brother of Yeshua?"

Ya'aqov nodded.

"Speak when you're spoken to by an official of the Roman government, Jewish shitbag!"

"I'm the Jewish shitbag you want," said Ya'aqov, squinting into the sun toward them. A second soldier dismounted and walked up within inches of his face.

"You make another comment like that, Jew, and I'll drag you back to Jerusalem behind my horse. Now get on before I run you through."

* * *

Ya'aqov sat silently on the horse, watching the circle of birds that followed them overhead. The horses panted and dripped foam from their mouths, struggling to stay cool enough to continue the journey. Every so often, one of the less sturdy men would grow faint and begin to slide from his mount, only to be met by a crack on the helmet by the flat side of another legionnaire's sword, rousing him back to consciousness.

"You must be someone of great interest to the Sanhedrin," said the legionnaire riding alongside Ya'aqov. "Ananus ben Ananus, your high priest, has requested an audience with you."

"He is not my high priest," Ya'aqov muttered.

"Might not want to start the conversation off with that bit of information," said the soldier. "A bit of sage advice that might help preserve your neck."

"The preservation of my neck does not concern me," said Ya'aqov.

"Oh? And what is more precious to you than your own life?"

"Truth."

"Truth!" the man laughed. "If you're gifted with such clarity as to claim the truth, why don't you share it with us, Jew?"

"You would not hear it if I did," he said.

23

"So, should I call you Mom or what?" said Jacob. His gaze jumped from the couch to the cluttered kitchen. He walked around the living area, hands shoved into his front pockets, studying photographs of Colette with her other children and past boyfriends.

"You can call me whatever," she smiled, gnawing at the edge of a fingernail. "Not like I exactly earned the title of 'mom,' but that's up to you, I guess."

"These kids," he pointed to a photograph of the boy and girl in their YMCA soccer uniforms, kneeling before a ball half their size. "I guess these are my half-brother and sister?"

"I hadn't thought about it, but yeah, I guess so," Colette said and walked over and smiled at the figures in the frame. "Adam there is seven. He's in second grade. Sophie's three. She's on one of those teams where they pretty much throw a ball out there and let 'em swarm around it like ants. I don't know if she's learning a damn thing, but she has fun."

"She's really cute."

"Yeah, she's a doll." Colette brushed some dust off the top of the picture. "Good thing, too. She's all piss and fire, that one. If she didn't have her looks going for her, I don't know if she'd make it in the world. Adam's a good boy. Always has been.

Likes to read. Doesn't have too many friends, but he seems to get on with the other kids at school all right. Sometimes they make fun of him for being poor, and nothing breaks my heart more than that, but he deals with it better than I do."

"I didn't have that problem growing up since we were all poor," said Jacob. "Got anything to drink?"

"Yeah," Colette went over and opened the door to the refrigerator. "I got some soda, a little bit of apple juice, some beer," she peered over the top of the door. "Does it make me a bad mom if I offer my teenage son a beer?"

"Not like I'm driving," said Jacob, sitting on a stool.

"Hope you like local stuff," she said, popping the cap off a bottle on the corner of the linoleum countertop. "I get a free case with every paycheck, so that's pretty much what I drink."

"Fine with me," he said, taking a swig and inspecting the label. "So you work there?" he said, pointing at a factory in the image on the bottle.

"Yep, for longer than I care to remember."

"That must be pretty cool," he said, "working in a place that makes beer."

"It's all right at first," she said and shrugged. "After a while, it's just another job like anywhere else." She leaned against the counter. "So what about you? What have you been up to since, well, birth?"

"What do you want to know?"

"Everything, I guess," she said. "But that'd probably keep us up all night."

"Not really," he said, taking a sip. "There's not that much to tell."

"Did I hear you say you're a musician?"

"Jazz mostly, yeah." He tapped out rhythms on the neck of

the bottle. "I got a horn from Scratch a long time ago, and just never put it down."

"That's so amazing," she said. "I have no musical talent at all."

"I must have gotten it from my dad," he smiled crookedly.

"This whole thing is so strange," she said, taking a deep breath.

"Tell me about it," said Jacob. "All of a sudden I'm the spawn of Jesus or something."

The pair shared a palpable silence. Colette pushed a rag across the counter in figure eights, and Jacob picked at the corner of the label on his beer.

"So you've actually had some amazing things happen."

"The bleeding and stuff?" said Jacob. "Mostly it was just annoying until the thing with Elena's scars, and even then, it didn't mean that much until Nica came along and told me I was a part of this genetic experiment thing—whatever." He took another swig. "It's kinda weird how different we look, huh? What about where you grew up?"

"Just up the road," she pointed at the north wall of her apartment. "Farm and ranch town. Pretty boring, really. My mom and dad are still up there on the same damn piece of dirt they've been on since I was born, and for all I know, they'll be buried there."

"That doesn't sound so bad," said Jacob, "knowing where you are every day when you wake up,, not having to worry about where to go or what to do. You can just, I don't know, be there."

"It is nice in the summer," she said and smiled wistfully. "Especially at night. The stars just blanket the whole sky. Talk about feeling small."

They fell into another uncomfortable silence until a muffled knock came at the front door. Colette opened it to find Nica holding a pair of plastic bags in one hand and a cardboard box in the other.

"Geez," said Jacob, standing to help her, "what all did you get?"

"Everything we need," she said, "which wasn't easy this time of night. I even found an all-night copy store to ship the sample off to Dr. Pavel."

"The genetics guy?"

"You got it," she set the box on the couch and the bags on the counter. She tossed a carton of cigarettes to Colette and a change of clothes to Jacob. "I hope those fit. There's not much of a selection in the middle of the night."

"Who the hell is Sean John?" he said, holding up an oversized red shirt decorated with a tilted crown and graffiti-style logo.

"Puff Daddy," said Nica. "Sean Combs. P-Diddy?"

"I have no idea who you're talking about," he said, sticking the shirt back in the bag, "but they must be some fat fuckers."

"It needs to be big," Nica said.

Jacob nodded. "Thanks," he said. "I didn't mean to sound ungrateful. This is actually the nicest thing anyone's bought me in a long time." Colette peered at the contents in the box.

"No problem. So how are you two getting on?"

"Oh, you know," said Colette, "getting to know each other, catching up a little bit."

"I hope I didn't interrupt."

"No, we're just talking," Jacob said. "Want a beer?" He looked at Colette. "Sorry, I guess I shouldn't offer stuff that's not mine."

"Hell, you're my kid," she said. "All that you see is yours."

"I'll take one, thanks." Nica sat down next to Jacob. "Did you get a chance to call Gus?"

"Shit, no," said Jacob. "I got all into talking and forgot. Jacob pulled his phone from his pocket and wandered down the hall with Colette's eyes following him until he disappeared around the corner.

"What an incredible kid," she said.

"He's great," said Nica. "Considering the circumstances, I think he's dealing with all of this pretty well."

"I just can't believe it's really him."

"We'll know more for sure by tomorrow night," said Nica. "The package will get there in about twenty-four hours, and once he has it, Pavel says he can run an analysis in less than an hour. He said he'd call me as soon as he knows something."

"It's funny," said Colette, "but there's little stuff he does, like how he smiles and other things when he's not thinking about it. I can see my dad in there."

"That would be strange."

"Your tests can say whatever they're gonna say, but I know in my heart, that's my kid."

"We'll consider the DNA test as backup," smiled Nica.

"I have to thank you for all of this." Colette's eyes glistened. "There have been so many times all these years that I've wondered what happened to that baby, and to have him standing here in my house, right in front of me..." She held a hand to her mouth.

Jacob reemerged from the bedroom.

"How'd it go with Gus?" Nica asked.

"He was kinda pissed about his place," said Jacob, sitting back on the stool. "I guess Haman knocked over some of his records and stuff. I explained to him what happened, though, the plan and everything. He was cool. He said he had a shipment set to go to a buyer in Florence tomorrow."

"Did he agree to the plan if we pick up the extra costs?" asked Nica.

"He said if you mention his store in your story, he'll write it all off as a business expense. He's loaded anyway. He just acts like he's poor."

"I guess that's it, then," said Nica. She looked at Jacob and Colette. "How about a toast," she said, raising her bottle. "To family."

"Sure, why not?" Colette smiled. "To family."

"That's not something I thought I'd ever say," shrugged Jacob. "But what the hell. To family."

24

"**B**ring him in," said Hillel. He was the Nasi presiding over the twenty-two other officials making up the Sanhedrin. Two priests returned with Ya'aqov, who was squinting and disoriented, and stood him in front of the expansive table where the council sat.

"Ya'aqov bar Yosef," said the Nasi, "you have been charged with capital crimes against Jewish law, including blasphemy. In addition, you are accused of lesser offenses including working on Shabbat, denigration of the temple leadership, insurrection, and violation of a number of kashrut dietary laws. How do you respond to these charges?"

"Does it matter how I respond?" he asked.

"Everyone is given an opportunity to speak on their own behalf, in the spirit of equitable justice."

"If equitable justice was involved," he said, "I would not have been brought before the Sanhedrin before standing trial in a lower court. Besides, where in Jewish law is it written that insurrection is an offense over which you have any jurisdiction?"

"You shall not question the authority of this council!" said Hillel. "You are here to explain your actions as a follower of Yeshua bar Yosef, the one who himself was found guilty of blasphemy."

"What act are you referring to that is so blasphemous?"

Ya'aqov said. "The fact that I witnessed my own brother perform miracles of healing, or that I promote his notions of love, forgiveness, and justice that are far more sovereign than those which you and your cohorts dole out as it pleases you?"

"The very fact that you do not recognize the sovereignty of this body," bellowed Hillel, "is itself an act of blasphemy! Have you nothing to say in your own defense, or are you so eager to be sentenced that you would have us dispatch with the formalities of considering your offenses with prudence?"

"You have no prudence," said Ya'aqov, "and in my eyes, you have no authority." He spat on the ground before him, eliciting gasps from the men around the table. "Sentence me as you already intend to do, and let's be done with this charade you consider to be prudent. The people of Jerusalem will see through your motives clearly enough, so there is nothing you can do to me. If you let me live, I will continue taking Yeshua's message to all who will hear it until my legs will no longer carry me. If you kill me, the people, upon whom you depend for the maintenance of order and your positions of power, will see to it that the prophecies are fulfilled, and that not one stone of this temple is left atop another."

"Then you are sentenced to death by stoning," howled Hillel, "when the sun reaches its zenith tomorrow. You are to be executed beyond the boundary of Jerusalem to avoid public skirmishes, and your remains will be handed over to your family for burial. May the Lord have mercy on your eternal soul, Ya'aqov bar Yosef. You have brought shame upon the heads of your family. Get him out of the temple!"

The priests escorted him back to his cell and slammed the door closed. From outside the door, the faint echo of laughter could be heard. It was a maniacal, defiant sort of laughter, growing in intensity, a shrill crescendo that carried through the narrow hallway and back into the great chamber where the Sanhedrin convened.

* * *

"Ya'aqov," the voice had stirred him from his fitful sleep on the cramped floor. "Open your eyes." Ya'aqov rose, searching the small space with his eyes for the source of the voice, but finding no one.

"Brother?" he whispered, his voice hoarse from his defiant display earlier. "Yeshua, is that you?"

"The time has come for you to rest," said the voice.

"Is that why you roused me? To tell me to rest?"

"Your work is done here," the voice said. "It is finished. You have served well."

"I fear for the lives of my children," said Ya'aqov, massaging a cramp out of his neck. "For Yehudah and his family. I fear for the well-being of all who cling to the message of hope we have brought to them. Have we condemned them to death? Have we made a difference at all?"

"If it were for you to do again," the voice said, "would you have lived differently?"

"I suppose not," he sighed, "but it's a struggle, committing yourself to a cause, without knowing the results that will follow."

"We threw ourselves into a call," the voice said, "not the result."

"Even as a disembodied voice," said Ya'aqov, "you still have sage advice. I shall enjoy sharing a few thoughts of my own about this movement of yours, perhaps over some wine and cheese in your Father's house."

"Not my Father, but ours. A place is set for you, my brother. Go in peace."

"Easy for you to say," said Ya'aqov. "You're already dead."

* * *

The next morning Ya'aqov was dragged from his cell by a wiry priest who looked perturbed. "Come along, you," he snarled, baring his teeth as he pulled Ya'aqov along. He took him to a small room in the back of the temple. He pointed to chair, upon which was draped a fresh tunic, next to a table with a basin of water, a cloth, and a small bowl of fruit. "Clean yourself," said the priest. "You stink of indignity. Fill your belly one last time, for what it's worth. I'll return for you shortly." He closed the door, leaving Ya'aqov alone.

Ya'aqov devoured the fruit, not having eaten the day before except for the pomegranate, and then gulped down half of the water in the basin before setting it back down and slumping into the chair. He ran his fingers along the hem of the garment, finely crafted with ornate trim. The material was of a superior quality to his own clothing.

"What a waste," he shook his head, "decorating myself in the most expensive clothes I've ever had, only to die in them."

He stripped off his old clothes and washed himself carefully, removing all remnants of the desert from his body. He performed ablutions, flushing his eyes, ears, nose, and mouth clean with water. As he lifted the tunic to wrap it around himself, a dove alighted on the ledge of the single small window, set high in the opposite wall. "You're the lucky one, you know," he said. "You'll never see yours coming. Count your ignorance among your blessings."

With his body refreshed and his hunger and thirst somewhat satiated, he knelt to pray. He rose from his prostrate position once he heard the door open behind them. He stood, and
without turning toward the figure at the door, he nodded.

"I am ready."

The ride to the outskirts of town was solemn. An occasional onlooker strained to see who the object of such grave attention was, but there were no crowds, as the Sanhedrin had not
announced Ya'aqov's trial publicly. Word would soon spread of
his trial absent of witnesses or requisite warnings under law
and of his execution, but for now the journey was eerily peaceful.

There would be protests, uprisings in several villages and
at the steps of the temple, and some would even say that it
was Ya'aqov's death that lit the spark leading to the first great
conflagration between the Jews and Romans—the Great War.
Some would shrink at the very mention of the names Ya'aqov
or Yeshua, dreadfully afraid of meeting a similar fate. Some
would even more passionately carry on the message following
Ya'aqov's death, but ultimately most of those would also join
him in meeting an untimely, violent death.

Many of the so-called dissident Jews who survived the purg-
ing saw the destruction of the great temple some years later
as penance for the opportunistic Sanhedrin who dispatched
Ya'aqov for the sake of preserving their own positions, and for
their concept of order and righteousness. A few of the more
fearful proclaimed the fledgling movement dead, hardly
before it had a chance to take hold. Others, including a few of
the Sanhedrin themselves, gained clarity about the intent of
Yeshua's ministry with some distance, committing themselves
to the cause that they had nearly helped undo.

The one they called Paulus Romanus, once a fierce slayer of many followers of Yeshua, ended up galvanizing the organizers of the small underground network of home churches, encouraging them in the wake of his passionate conversion to lay down their own lives for what they believed, just as the brothers of Yosef had done before them.

Nearly three centuries later, the Roman emperor Flavius Constantinus, known as Augustus to his many legions, put an end to the bloody persecution of Christians, adopting the faith as the official religion of the state, and his legacy was carried out by generations succeeding him. The reach of the Christian faith would stretch into what would become Europe, South America, and to all corners of the world, sometimes by force and sometimes by grace, until hardly a soul breathed that had not heard the story of Yeshua bar Yosef of Nazareth.

But Ya'aqov only saw his fate in the form of a handful of blunt stones handed out to a crowd hungry for blood and silver. For each in the circle, a single coin was placed in one hand. In the other was laid a stone, until all who stood around him bore the weight of both.

No one would volunteer to participate in the execution, so the legionnaires rounded up beggars, lepers, and madmen, eager to earn a meager wage. They stood around him like a seething pack of rabid dogs, poised to vent their anger at the whole world upon the man bound to a pole before them, whose transgressions they did not know or care to understand. As one of the guards tightened the knots of the straps around Ya'aqov's wrists, a particularly agitated bystander hurled his stone prematurely, striking the soldier on the temple, bringing him to his knees. Two of his Roman cohorts dragged the bystander from the circle, bludgeoning him with several sound blows to the head as blood gushed from his mouth.

Once the excitement was quelled, the Centurion overseeing the procedure walked into the center of the crowd and stood before Ya'aqov. He unrolled a scroll and cleared his throat.

"People of Jerusalem, by decree from the holy council of your own Sanhedrin, Ya'aqov bar Yosef, the Nazarene, is sentenced to death by stoning for blasphemy. He was handed over to the procurator and his legion to carry out the orders of execution on this day under the height of the sun. If anyone here wishes to register an objection or complaint regarding this charge or the subsequent sentence to be entered into the official record, let him speak now."

The unruly crowd stared, beady eyed, in silence, raising their stones in anticipation of the signal.

"So be it," proclaimed the Centurion, rolling up the scroll and tucking it under his arm. He exited the circle and signaled to his legionnaire to continue.

The young man unsheathed his sword, raised it high above him, and as he brought it to the ground the stones rained in, converging on the body before them in a dull chorus of thuds and cracks, soon rendering Ya'aqov lifeless.

25

"You keep an eye on her," Haman pointed at Elena. "I have to make a call." She was strapped to an armchair, bound from behind the neck with duct tape on top of a cloth that was stuffed into her mouth. Though Elena could make no sound, her facial expressions suggested she was choking on the rag.

"Isn't there some other way we could deal with this?" asked Scratch, uncomfortably watching her face. "This hardly seems necessary."

"That's not your concern," said Haman, picking up the phone. "It's clear to me that you've become far too emotionally involved with this assignment. It was simply your job to keep the boy alive and to report any signs. To this point, you've done that, if less than professionally, so I suggest you keep your mouth shut and do as you're told."

Haman dialed the phone while watching Scratch closely. Elena looked at the priest with a mix of confusion and despair. He wanted to reassure her, to apologize for his part in her capture and ransom, but fear kept him silent.

"Haman here," he said. "Tell the Bishop we'll be bringing the boy in tonight. I'll call again if there are any problems, but we're just waiting here. He's coming to us." Haman's face grew more severe as the voice on the other end went on. "Look," he said, closing his eyes, "I don't tell you how to do your job, do I? Then don't tell me how to do mine. I'm doing what I was sent here to do. The rest is not for you to worry about. Just tell the Bishop like I said."

He hung up the phone and sat down behind Scratch's desk. He pulled a nine-millimeter Ruger pistol from his jacket pocket, set it on the desk, and grabbed a full clip from his other pocket. Sliding the clip into its place in the handle of the gun, he pressed the bottom with the heel of his hand, setting the clip into its final position.

"What in the hell do you need that for?" Scratch's eyes widened. Elena let out a faint grunt from behind the gag. "You said you told him to come unarmed, and Jacob's not a violent kid. Why not just explain to him that he's a part of something incredible, something that could change the whole world? Why not at least start by trying to reason with him instead of resorting to all of these barbaric coercion tactics? After all, you said yourself, he's no good to The Project if he dies."

"That's true," said Haman, "but what happens after I bring the boy in is none of my business. It's my job to bring him to the Bishop. If I can't do that, I have orders to make sure no one else finds out that this program ever existed."

"And what is that supposed to imply?" said Scratch. "Are you suggesting that you'll kill both of us if Jacob doesn't cooperate?"

"You know too much as it is," said Haman. "Even if he does cooperate, I have no idea what the Bishop has planned for you."

"I don't understand how you can be so clinical and removed about this," said Scratch. "Here we have one chance to change the entire course of history. This young man possesses the key to the hastening of the second coming, and you treat him as if he's just another target, or a package to be delivered to its final destination."

"Look," said Haman as he inspected the chamber of the Ruger, "we've been working on this for more than twenty years. People have gone to great lengths to secure the genetic materials necessary for this program. Many have invested their lives to ensure that this was carried out to its necessary completion. Do you know how much easier it would have been to raise this boy ourselves, to keep the rest of the world from corrupting him with their vile culture of greed and hedonism? I tried to tell the Bishop that we were giving up too much control this way, but he was convinced, by a vision, that the boy had to live in the world, and that if he truly was who we hoped he would be, the signs would become more than evident.

"It's not my call to decide what the right kind of evidence is. I follow orders. You could learn something from that, you know. You think I'm some empty-headed idiot, doing as I'm told, but what you don't seem to get is that this world works only when there's a proper order to things."

"I understand Jacob's purpose," said Scratch, "but it was always my understanding that he was to come to realize his power and his divinity on his own, if indeed it was within him. Now we're talking about sequestering him, testing him like a laboratory animal, and forcing him to do our bidding? This is not what I agreed to."

"Let me tell you a little story," said Haman, putting his feet up on Scratch's desk. "Once upon a time, there was a man who was drowning at sea. In a moment of desperation, he cried out to God to save him. After a while, a boat comes by and tries to throw him a life preserver, but the man declines. 'I'm a man of faith,' he says, 'and I'm waiting for God to save me.' A little while later, the waters are getting rough and the sun is starting to go down. The man is shaking from the cold, barely able to keep his head above water when another boat comes by. The crew on board tries to toss him a line but again the man refuses. 'God will save me,' he says. 'I have faith!' Soon after that the man drowns. His soul ascends to heaven, and as he stands before God, he cries out, 'Why didn't you save me, God? I prayed for your deliverance, and you just let me die!' A little annoyed, God leans down toward the man and says, 'What do you want from me? I sent you two boats!'" Haman cackled dryly to himself, polishing the top of the gun with his sleeve.

"I know you're insane," said Scratch, "but I have no idea what you're getting at, if, in fact, there is a point."

"The point is, you intellectual maggot, that this whole planet is drowning in its own filth. We're poisoning our air until we can't breathe. We'll pollute our water until there's not a drop left to drink. Meanwhile, we pray to God for deliverance from our own squalor. But what we fail to understand is our own agency in the whole plan of salvation. Science, ironically, is at the very heart of salvation. While everyone debates whether or not Adam and Eve roamed the earth with dinosaurs, or whether the planet is twenty billion years old, both sides are missing the point. God is speaking to us. He's given us everything we need, right here. How else do you think we were able to secure DNA that was two thousand years old? To employ the scientific tools necessary to rebuild an ancient puzzle and fit it into the womb of a young woman, just like the story of Jesus Christ himself? It's the fulfillment of the final prophecies. This is the End of Days, and the key to unlocking the gates has been placed in our hands!"

"You're right!" a voice called from the church sanctuary. "I'm here."

Haman and Scratch passed through the walkway into the worship chamber where they found Jacob leaning against the outside of the arm rail of the choir loft, his feet clinging to the thin lip of wood extending from the floor.

"Jacob," said Scratch, "what are you doing?"

"Listening," said Jacob, "for a while now. That's quite a plan you guys have, taking me hostage, killing all the witnesses, having your way with me like I was a slab of fucking meat." He adjusted his collar to reveal a thick rope around his neck, fastened into the form of a noose which dangled behind him.

"Jacob, no…"

"Shut up!" Jacob cried. Tears streamed from his face, dripping down onto the hardwood floor more than fifteen feet below. "You've had your chance to talk. Now it's my turn. Where's Elena?"

"She's in the office," said Haman, his hand firmly pressed into his jacket pocket. "No one is here to hurt you, and as long as you do as we ask, no harm will come to her."

"Right," said Jacob, "and why the hell should I believe you?"

"You have no choice but to believe me," said Haman.

"That's where you're wrong," said Jacob. "See, I got to thinking about something that Scratch said the other day in his office. He said something about how I wouldn't be any good to you dead. At first I didn't want to believe there was anything weird about it, but after a while, I realized that it meant he had to be in on this too. He'd been talking to somebody who was telling him what to do. I guess I should be grateful they need me alive, huh Scratch?"

"Jacob, I'm so sorry."

"No, I'm sorry!" He yelled, his foot slipping from the railing, before he regained his balance. "I'm sorry for ever trusting you. I'm sorry for being stupid enough to walk right into your fucking trap, telling you everything you wanted to know. I'm sorry I ever tried to think I could love you like a father. You were God to me, Scratch. But at least now I know where I stand." Scratch lowered his head, holding his face in his hands.

"Turns out, though," said Jacob, "that your little screw up was a real favor to me. See, I've always wondered where I came from and what the hell I was supposed to do with my life. Then I find out my whole existence is some friggin' joke, some game for your twisted amusement. Well, I may not have control over much in the world, but I do have some power left over what happens with my own life." Jacob stood up, his hands clinging to the railing behind him.

"Please, Jacob, stop," Scratch pleaded. "This doesn't have to happen."

"Yeah?" said Jacob, looking down at the floor below. "Tell me how that's going to work. If I agree to go with him, there's no way he's going to let Elena go. She knows too much. And you've already clearly fucked me over, so who the hell else do I have?"

"What about your mother?"

"Oh yeah, her. You mean the woman I met yesterday? We haven't exactly had much time to get reacquainted. If you're shipping me off to God-knows-where to make me a part of your experiment, what does it matter?"

"Jacob, listen," said Scratch, reaching his hand out toward him. "You know that suicide is a mortal sin."

"Don't you fucking talk to me about sin," Jacob yelled. "You hypocrite! What do you know about other peoples' sin! How can you even call yourself a priest, let alone my friend?"

"Oh, I believe you still have feelings for Father William," Haman raised the gun to Scratch's temple. "Now, why don't you come down from there, and we'll talk this through. I think there's been a gross misunderstanding. You have a very special place in the faith. You are the one who will bring about the new order, the one that will set everything right again. I see it in you. You are the Promised One, Jacob. The world needs you. And at the moment," he said, pressing the gun harder against Scratch's head, "he needs you too. You may be angry at him, but you love him, and you don't want to see him die."

Jacob stared at Scratch, who was now on his knees in front of Haman, weeping. "You're right," said Jacob, "I don't want to see it." As he released the railing, his body fell forward, arms outstretched, until gravity swept his feet from the ledge. The fall was silent until his body expended the full length of rope, causing it to snap wildly and recoil several feet up in the air, contorting Jacob's body with his arms and legs in front of him. As the rope extended again, Jacob's body hung lifeless from the rope, spinning slowly clockwise and then back again.

"My God," whispered Father William, "what have we done?"

"This is not about us," said Haman, standing over Scratch. "This is about you. You've failed at your mission. You've failed the Bishop, and you've failed God." Haman pulled the top of the gun back, allowing a bullet to settle into the chamber, placed the butt of the barrel on the back of Scratch's head, and pulled the trigger.

Elena had been straining to decipher the commotion around the strips of tape covering most of her ears, but the echo of the gunshot caused her to seize against her bonds. She wept quietly as she waited for someone to round the corner, wailing louder as the only face she saw was Haman's.

"Your boyfriend made a very poor choice, dear," Haman said grimly, raising the gun to meet her forehead. Elena shut her eyes tightly, waiting for permanent darkness to set in when she heard a sound like splintering wood, followed by the dull thud of a body in front of her. She opened her eyes to find Nica standing with Jacob's skateboard in her hands, blood on the trucks and wheels beneath, and Haman's motionless body at her feet.

26

"What a fucking mess," said Nica, dropping the board to the side. "Let's get you out of this chair."

Nica cut the tape and cords with a pair of scissors from the desk and pulled Elena to her feet. She was trembling so severely she had trouble standing on her own, so Nica draped Elena's arm over her shoulder. From the other room came a shrill yelp, followed by another thud and the sound of furniture falling.

"What the hell was that?" said Elena, pulling her hair back from her face.

"Sounded like Colette cutting him loose," said Nica. He's probably not feeling too good right about now." They returned to the sanctuary where Jacob was gingerly lifting himself out of a pile of chairs and a small table that had previously held holy water.

"Holy shit," Jacob wheezed, "you didn't tell me that would hurt so bad."

"Sorry," said Nica. "I'm sure if Frederick had been here to set the harness himself, it wouldn't have been quite as bad, but I had no idea what I was doing."

Jacob pulled his shirt up to reveal a red canvas harness that ran between his legs, twice across his chest and over his shoulders. The rope was affixed to the harness between his shoulders, with the frayed end dragging on the floor between his feet.

"I think I cracked a rib," he groaned, "and I twisted my ankle when she cut me loose."

"Sorry, honey," Colette said from the balcony. She put the knife back in her pocket and headed for the stairs that led her back down into the sanctuary. "That's what Nica said to do."

"What's going on, Jacob?" Elena stammered.

She looked toward the body, lying in a pool of blood on the floor. "Oh God," she said in a hushed voice, "is that Scratch?" Jacob's attention changed from his bruised chest to the priest. He walked toward the body and stood for a moment over it. Kneeling down, he placed his hands on Scratch's back and lowered his head.

"Fucking Scratch," he cried under his breath. "Why? Why the hell did he have to be a part of this?"

Elena came to his side, placing a comforting arm around him. Jacob lifted one hand above his head and, clenching it tightly into a fist, brought it down heavily on the priest's back. "I love you, you stupid son of a bitch! Didn't you know that? Didn't you know?" He collapsed, sobbing on top of the only man he thought of as a father, the first person he thought of as a friend, and a symbol of the possibility of the Divine in flesh, snuffed out like the simple, frail man that he actually was.

Jacob clawed at the black vestments as he wailed, bringing Elena to sympathetic tears alongside him. He shook his head in mournful denial, as if to ward off the inevitable by an act of sheer will. "Don't die, dammit," he whispered. "Please don't die."

A gurgling noise came from beneath the body, followed by a jarring gasp. Jacob fell back as Scratch lurched, his chest rising and falling as if he were underwater, yearning for the surface.

"Quick, roll him over," said Nica. "I think he's alive." Jacob and Elena stared at the undead priest, writhing like a serpent. "He's choking, Jacob! Get him out of the blood!" Jacob blinked at Nica, pulling himself from his stupor enough to push Scratch out of the pool of his own fluids and onto his side. The priest gasped, his lips dripping with crimson droplets, and he opened his eyes.

"Jesus," said Jacob. "Scratch?" The priest looked wildly around the room, his eyes finally training on the source of the voice.

"Jacob," he said, his voice thick and wet, "you're alive."

"Me?" said Jacob. "What about you? That guy shot you, point-blank, right in the back of the skull." Scratch reached for the back of his head, searching for signs of a wound.

"Maybe he missed."

"He didn't fucking miss, man. Look at the floor. That's your blood!"

"I don't know what to tell you," Scratch sat up slowly, "but I seem to be alive. I remember the gun going off, and then everything went black. The next thing I knew, I heard your voice, calling me to you, and here I am."

"Jesus, Mary, and Joseph," Colette dropped to her knees. "It's a miracle. Jacob, you did it."

"Did what?" said Jacob. "I just asked him not to die, is all."

"Well whatever you did," said Nica, "it seems to have worked." She looked toward Scratch's office. "I hate to be pushy, but the bad guy is going to be waking up soon, and I'm not sure it's a good idea for Jacob to still be here."

"She's right," said Scratch. "You should go."

"What about you?"

"I can handle him," said Scratch, rising to his feet. "I'd like to see his reaction when he comes to and looks me in the eye. Don't worry about me." Jacob grabbed him and held him tightly.

"You know," he said, "whatever happened is done. I love you, Scratch. I can't help it." Scratch buried his face in Jacob's shoulder and wept tears of relief and joy, finally pushing him away.

"I love you, too," he said, wiping his eyes. "That's why I'm telling you to get the hell out of here, now."

Nica pulled the car around from behind the church. Jacob and Elena got in the back seat, and Colette sat next to Nica in front. "Here are two one-way tickets," said Nica, "courtesy of your friend and employer, Gus."

"Cool," said Jacob, pulling the boarding passes out of the sleeve. "I've never been on a plane before."

"This will be quite a first trip," Colette said.

"What about the albums?" Elena asked.

"In a box in the trunk," said Nica. "Gus said he told a client in Florence that you would be the couriers and to meet you at the other end to take them off your hands. I have two duffel bags for both of you back there, too. Just the basics: toiletries, a change of clothes, that kind of thing. Your plane leaves in less than an hour and a half, so we have to keep moving." She reached into the console between her and Colette, producing a slim, white envelope. "This is a little something from me." She smiled. Jacob pulled five one hundred dollar bills from inside.

"Shit," he said, inspecting the currency. "I haven't seen that much money in one place before."

"This is a day of firsts," she said, "for all of us, I think. You guys don't have passports, right?" Jacob and Elena looked at each other. "You can travel to the Caribbean without one, and when you get there, you'll meet a guy named Philip. He'll get you set up with the paperwork you need."

"How do you know this kind of crazy shit?" said Jacob.

"Let's just say I've done a little bit of traveling in my years as a reporter," she said, "and sometimes it's helpful to travel under the radar."

"You're amazing, you know that?" Elena grabbed her tightly.

"You'd better get going," said Nica. "You're on a tight schedule."

* * *

"I hope you have something interesting to tell me," grumbled Edward, "calling me in the middle of the night."

"I'll explain everything tomorrow," Nica said, "but I probably won't be in first thing in the morning."

"You still in Denver?"

"For a few more minutes," she said. "I have the next flight out."

"Good," he sighed. "My week has been boring as hell around here without you."

"Wish I could say the same."

"By the way," said Edward, "some kraut called for you just before I left the office. Said to tell you that the sample was a match."

"No shit."

* * *

Haman slowly lifted his throbbing head, his eyes finally focusing on the barrel of his own gun, trained on a point in the middle of his forehead.

"Nice nap?" said Scratch, pressing the end of the gun against Haman's flesh. Haman reflexively tried to raise his hands in protection, but they were bound with a nylon cord to the arms of the same chair to which he had tied Elena.

"You," he stammered, breathless and still disoriented from the blow to his head. "But I…"

"Killed me?" Scratch smiled. "Would have thought so, at such close range. Good thing for me I had the boy wonder around."

"Where is he?" growled Haman, his wrists straining against the rope. "If you let him go, God help you when the Bishop finds out."

Scratch chuckled dryly.

"Given the current arrangement, and seeing as I'm the only one here who has recently been raised from the dead, I'd say God and I are in a good place. And as for Jacob, you don't have to worry about him. He's beyond your reach by now."

"No one is beyond the Bishop's reach," said Haman, a sneer creeping over his mottled face. "It's only a matter of time."

"You listen to me, shit for brains," said Scratch, leaning in next to Haman's ear. "There's only one reason you're still alive."

"Yeah," said Haman, "what's that?"

"I want you to deliver a message to the Bishop for me." Scratch leaned across to his desk and plucked up the letter opener with his free hand. Haman's breath quickened as Scratch raised the glinting tip of the blade beneath his chin. "You tell him I'm done with him and his project. You tell him if any of his people come around here again, someone won't leave alive. Tell him whatever Jacob is, or is still becoming, it is way more than he bargained for. And you tell him if he knows what's best for all involved, he'll let the boy go and pretend none of this ever took place."

"You really think the Bishop would give up on a project this important just because some weak-willed priest tossed around a handful of empty threats?" Haman said, shaking his head, his eyes still fixed on Scratch. "This is his destiny, and it's my destiny to help him. I thought it was yours as well, but I can see now we were wrong about you. You might as well kill me now, because if you let me go, you're a dead man."

"You already tried that, remember?" Scratch lowered the blade, inserting it between Haman's right wrist and the rope holding him fast.

With a few sawing motions, he cut Haman's arm free, pausing with the letter opener hovering over his other wrist. "Now, the way I see it, you have two choices. You can either walk out of here after I cut you loose and go tell your boss what I told you, or you can take a bullet here in this chair and be seen as a failure by everyone involved in The Project. Me, I have nothing to lose. I already died once today. You want to give it a try, or are you going to think for once?" Haman sighed, wiping beads of sweat from his face with his free hand.

"Do you even know how to fire a gun?"

"Make a move and we'll both find out," said Scratch. "The cops should be here in a minute or two, so I recommend you choose quickly."

The faint howl of sirens seeped into the church. Haman glanced nervously toward the door.

"So you're just going to let me go," said Haman. "Why?"

"Aside from the message I want you to deliver?" said Scratch, cutting Haman's other hand loose. "Killing isn't really my thing. I'm a priest, remember?"

"Sure," said Haman, "you're practically a saint."

★ ★ ★

"I had no idea there would be so many seats in these things," said Elena, standing on her toes to look all the way to the back of the cabin.

"It's a little creepy," said Jacob, "all closed in like this. But I guess considering the day we've had, it's no big deal, really." They settled into their seats, grabbing each other's hands tightly as the plane rolled back from the gate.

A few minutes into the air, a flight attendant took their drink orders.

"I'll take a beer," said Jacob in an artificially deep voice, "if you have change for a hundred."

"Of course, sir," she smiled. "And you, miss?"

"Just a Sprite for me, thanks."

"Really?" Jacob looked at Elena. "I figured you'd want something to take the edge off after all the excitement. I heard they'll serve you 'till you pass out once you're headed for international waters."

"I don't think I should," said Elena.

"Why not? I've seen you throw down before."

"You know when I went back to Gus's place to take a nap?"

"Sure," said Jacob.

"Well, I wasn't exactly tired," Elena bit her lip. "I had to check something."

"I'm totally lost," Jacob said. "If you're trying to tell me something, just come out and say it."

"Jacob," Elena looked into his eyes, "I'm pregnant."

Special thanks to the following supporters
who helped bring *Blood Doctrine* **to life:**

Amy Sheppard
Bill Ecklund, M.D.
Carol Howard Merritt
Chris Jones
Cyrus White
Doc Edlin
Eric Elnes
My father, Frank Piatt
Gene and Bonnie Frazier
Harold Elias-Perciful
Hollie Woodruff
Jacques MacDonald
Jamie and Judy Frazier
Janet and Dirk Edwards
Jennifer Dawn Watts
Jon E. Smith
John & Mary Anne McComb
Kathryn A. Helmers

Laura Kay Rand
Liz Lazar-Johnson
Mark and Mary Kay Pumphrey
Matthew
Matt Slay
Mike McHargue
Paul Svenson
Rachel Frey
Rebecca Hardin-Nieri
Robert Fugarino
Ryan Kuramitsu
Sandra Nickel
Scott Arthur
Shelley Story
Susan Wolf
Suzie Frazier and Russ Shinn
Tormey

And to the more than 150 other backers
who supported this project, thank you!